THE LIES THAT BIND

A SEASIDE COTTAGE BOOKS COZY MYSTERY

KAREN MACINERNEY

GRAY WHALE PRESS

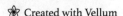 Created with Vellum

1

There is nothing more perfect than a Maine summer day, when the sun is bright in the sky, the water is the color of cobalt, and the breeze is perfumed with the scent of salt air tinged with roses.

It was my first summer back in Maine since I was a child, and every day I woke up enchanted once again by the sound of the bell buoy in the distance, the cries of the gulls above the harbor, and the low grumble of lobster boats heading out for the day. Now, as I put a pan of Mississippi Mud Bars into the oven and glanced out the window at the bright morning, I thanked my lucky stars once again that I'd managed to find my way back to my favorite childhood haunt, Snug Harbor.

I had an hour before the bookstore I'd recently bought, Seaside Cottage Books, opened: enough time for a walk while the brownie base of the bars I'd just made cooled. I gave my customers a free cookie with every purchase, which meant I got to spend a lot of time experimenting in the kitchen. It was a fun idea, but a couple of months into owning the business, I was realizing I was going to have to expand my marketing beyond the kitchen to bring more customers in.

I sprinkled mini marshmallows over the warm brownies and popped them back in the oven, setting the timer for three minutes. As the marshmallows puffed, I grabbed my shoes and the leash from the hook by the door, calling Winston, my rescue Bichon Frisé, who was still snoozing in a sunbeam on my bed.

"Come on, lazybones," I called as I walked into the bedroom, the wood floors creaking under my feet. Winston rolled on his back, presenting his tummy, and tilted his head. "No, you don't get to stay here. We both need our exercise!"

By the time I managed to wrangle him into a leash and into the living room, the timer had gone off, and I pulled the pan of brownies—now with a puffy marshmallow top— back out of the oven and put it on a rack to cool while we walked. I'd finish it with a thick, fudgy frosting and try not to eat half the pan before the store opened. This particular recipe was popular with both the customers and me, and I'd made several batches over the past few weeks.

I had opened the back door and was coaxing a reluctant Winston down the steps to the beach path when my phone rang. I picked up as I got to the bottom of the steps; it was my friend Denise, who managed Sea Beans coffee shop.

"Got some free time this afternoon?" she asked.

"I do, actually," I said. My assistant, Bethany, and my daughter, Caroline, were scheduled to take over the store from two to closing. "What did you have in mind?"

"I need to run something by you, and I thought maybe we could go blueberry picking and talk."

"Everything okay?"

"It is," she said. "I just... I'm not sure what to do about something. I can't go into it now, but can I pick you up?"

"I'll be free at two," I said.

"I'll swing by then," she said. "Thanks."

"I'm looking forward to it," I told her, and hung up, wondering what she needed to talk about. Last I'd heard, business was good at the coffee shop, and the staff was doing great, but as I was quickly learning, all kinds of things could come up when you ran a small business. Low sales, for example, I thought with a twinge of worry. My last month's receipts had been about twenty percent short of what I'd hoped, and since summer was the big season in Snug Harbor, I really needed to find a way to get customers in the door. As we walked down the path to the beach, I glanced over my shoulder at the cottage, which was nestled among trees at the top of a gentle hill. Although I loved that the store was a little off the beaten path—I didn't have to listen to the questionable live music acts at some of the restaurants closer to the center of Snug Harbor's lively downtown —traffic was definitely lighter than it would be if I were on the main street. I enjoyed lovely views of Snug Island and the harbor, instead of the back of another building, but the downside was that fewer people made it out to the fringes to shop and look for souvenirs. Was there some way to get customers to walk down to Seaside Cottage Books? I wondered.

I'd have to pick Denise's brain about it, I decided as I brushed past the blooming roses—I still marveled at their deep magenta petals and winy scent—and paused as Winston decided to relieve himself on a rounded hump of granite.

The morning was fresh and clean and new. As I got to the beach, Winston sniffing busily and trailing just a bit behind me, I turned toward town, eyes sweeping the wet pebbly beach, looking, as always, for gleaming chunks of sea glass. As I walked toward town, I could hear the sound of dishes clattering from one of the several restaurants that backed the harbor, along with the low call of a horn as one of the bigger tourist boats left the dock—I was guessing it might be one of the birdwatching cruises, or a whale watch. Whale-watching was on my bucket list for the summer. I'd heard one or two occasionally came close to shore, and I'd spotted a few porpoises and dolphins in the harbor—always a thrill—but there was something magical about seeing those massive creatures slipping through the water. It always amazed me to think that they lived in another world, so close to and yet so far from our own.

Winston tugged at the leash, bringing me back to the beach; at the same time, I spotted a gleam of white against the gray of the rocks and the blue of broken mussel shells. I stooped down to pick up what looked like the delicate handle of a cup, smoothed with age; a part of the cup still attached to the graceful arch of white china. Who had sipped from this cup? And how had it ended up tumbled on the ocean's floor?

I was full of dreamy ideas today, I thought as I tucked the treasure into my pocket. If only I could translate some of them into profitable action items. The anxiety over my business made me hungry for chocolate, or maybe a piece of coffee cake from Sea Beans, but even small extravagances weren't in the budget at the moment. I'd have to settle for a Mississippi Mud Bar when I got home. Not that that was by any means a sacrifice.

A cool breeze ruffled Winston's fur as he and I clambered over one of the granite boulders near the dock. Barnacles encrusted the weather-beaten piers, and seagulls called overhead, searching for an opportunity to grab a snack from an unwary tourist.

As I picked my way through the granite boulders with Winston at my side, a voice drifted over from the shore path above us. "What are you going to do with the body?"

I perked up.

"I figure we can weight it down and sink it," a second voice replied.

I looked up to see who it was, but a clump of rosebushes obscured my view. It was definitely a man and a woman.

"We want it to turn up, though," the woman said

"True," he acknowledged. "Maybe we don't bother moving it."

"It depends on where we do it," she said. "And how."

As they spoke, I crept to one side, hoping to find a gap in the bushes. I caught a glimpse of brown hair glinting in the sunlight, and maybe a blue shirt, but that was it. How was I going to find out who these people were?

"Poison?' he suggested

"How would we get it to her?"

"True," the man said. "It bears thinking about. We have time."

"Not too much, though," the woman warned. "We've got to get on with it."

"All unpleasant tasks grow when you put them off," he said. "I guess you're right." As he spoke, I could hear the voice drifting away; I'd gone the wrong direction. I made a sharp turn and hurried to the other end of the rosebushes, hoping to catch a glimpse of the pair, but Winston darted in front of me as I was about to jump to another rock. I spun in mid-air, trying not to squash him, and my foot slid between two rocks, wrenching sideways. I yelped and sat down hard, then pushed myself back up, testing my foot gingerly as

2

I unlocked the front door of the bookstore at ten. I'd wrapped my ankle, iced it, and taken Ibuprofen. Although it wasn't just like new, it was definitely feeling a little bit better. With Winston at my heels, I hobbled down the front walk with the blackboard easel advertising free cookies; I was hoping to lure passersby into the shop. Caroline pulled up in her car as I finished setting it up, waving as she turned into the driveway. I'd just limped back into the store when my daughter came through the back door, to be just about bowled over by an ecstatic Winston.

"Did you miss me, buddy?" she asked, squatting down and letting him cover her face with kisses. Her reddish-brown hair was braided, little tendrils escaping and curling in wisps against her pale skin; looking at her with Winston, I felt a wave of love for the young woman who used to be my baby girl. Then she scooped him up and hugged him. "Who's my best boy?"

"He loves having you in town," I said, feeling my heart swell with love at the sight of my nineteen-year-old daughter, whose face was now being bathed in kisses by Winston.

"You need a bath!" she said as he wriggled in her arms.

"I know," I said. "If you're up for it, I'd love it."

"Maybe once I've had breakfast," she said. "I picked up a bagel for you. Everything, right? With scallion cream cheese."

"Thanks. I call it the 'Date Repeller Bagel,'" I joked. Her face stiffened, and I regretted the comment immediately. My divorce from her dad was still fresh, and Caroline was having a hard time adjusting. Ted, my "wusband," had been seeing a glamorous bestselling author for several months now; she was spending so much time at Ted's house in Boston that Caroline had decided to move to Snug Harbor so she wouldn't be confronted with the new reality every day. Now that I was seeing Nicholas Waters, whom I'd had a crush on twenty-five years earlier when I spent summers in Snug Harbor, it was getting a bit awkward for me, too. I was almost glad my small apartment didn't have room to house my daughter; she was bunking with my mother, whose house wasn't far away.

"I'm supposed to be going blueberry picking this afternoon,' I said, attempting to change the subject. "Maybe you can make that lemon blueberry Bundt cake you made last summer?"

"Maybe," she said, but the enthusiasm I'd briefly seen was gone. That seemed to be the case in general for Caroline right now; I was beginning to wonder if she should see someone. While her twin, Audrey, seemed to be adjusting well, my normally bright and energetic Caroline was not. She was taking a "gap year" from college, but she didn't seem to have much of a plan, and seemed somehow to be adrift. She was working part-time for me, being trained by my assistant, Bethany, and theoretically looking for another job; unfortunately, until sales picked up, I couldn't afford to hire her full-time.

"How's the signing scheduling going, by the way?"

"I've got a local author scheduled for this Friday. Janice Morton's her name; she writes a series of mysteries set in Acadia National Park. Bethany ordered the books, and they should be here Thursday."

"That sounds fun," I said. "I've never heard of her before. Are the books good?"

"I don't know," she said. "We e-mailed, and she said she was available, so we went for it. Bethany wrote a press release and is sending it to the paper. Have you put up the Facebook page for the bookstore yet?"

"Not yet," I said. It was on the list of things that needed doing, but something about having to keep up with a social media page made me nervous. "Do you think you might take a crack at it?"

She brightened a bit. "Actually, that might be fun. Can I try?"

"That would be great," I said. "We probably have to post things every day, though."

"How about a picture of Winston with a new book every week?" she suggested. "Or a picture of the cookies you've got available?"

"That's a terrific idea!" I said. "I really need to do something to boost sales. I love our location, but we're a bit off the beaten path. We should probably sit down and brainstorm ways to get more customers in the door."

"Have you considered selling something other than books?"

"Um... it's a bookstore," I pointed out.

"I know," she said. "But... I don't know. Souvenirs. Locally made crafts. Maybe some Maine-based blank books, and pens, and balsam sachets with quotes from Maine writers."

"That's really creative," I said, but inside, I was wondering how to afford to buy all that merchandise.

"You could sell some of the stuff on consignment," she suggested, as if reading my mind. "And I can get some fabric printed with the quotes and do some of the sachet sewing myself. Maybe start a cottage business."

"It's worth a shot," I said, wondering at this change in my daughter. It had been this way recently: spurts of enthusiasm followed by apathy. Would this one last? "How do we find the people who do crafts?"

"Put it on the Facebook page," she suggested. "Say you're taking applications for people who want to sell things at the store. You take a cut, and if you have enough unusual things in here, it makes us more of a destination."

"I don't want to be a craft store though," I said. "I still want to be a bookstore."

"Of course, Mom," she said. "How about groups?"

"What do you mean, groups? Bethany's got a mystery writing group that meets every week."

"Yes, but what about a book club? Maybe you could order special copies—signed, even—from the publishers. If you host it, people would come here, talk about the book, browse, and maybe buy some more books." She bit her lip. "It would really create a community. You might even put a cafe in here..."

"All right, all right," I said, putting my hands up; the suggestions were overwhelming, but I was thrilled to see a spark of enthusiasm in my daughter's eyes. "I love all these ideas—they're amazing—but let's stick to one project at a time. As for a cafe? I barely have room for the books, much less a cafe."

"You'd have to build an addition. Or maybe put some of it upstairs."

"And live in a tent in the back yard," I joked.

"The building next door is for lease," she pointed out. The small shingle-style shop next door had been through multiple incarnations over the years; when I was a kid in Snug Harbor, it had been an ice cream store and an art gallery. Until recently, it had been a T-shirt store, but the owner had closed up shop at about the same time I moved to town. I hoped Seaside Cottage Books wouldn't follow suit.

"Let's start with a Facebook page," I said. Renting a building and adding on space was definitely out of the question, particularly with the balance of the store's books already in the red. "And write down all those ideas. I love your creativity... thank you so much for helping!"

"I'll get right on it," she said.

"I'm going to finish frosting the Mississippi Mud Bars now that they've cooled off," I said. "Can you keep an eye on things down here?"

"Yes... but let's get a good picture of those. They'll be our first Facebook post!"

I'D ICED and cut the bars (the fudge frosting was divine) and laid them on a pretty blue and white plate for Caroline to snap a few shots—she put a rose in front of the plate, to "style" it, and an open book beside it—and was stealing one for myself when two men walked into the shop, casting a speculative eye around at the sea glass-filled mason jars on the windowsills, the wooden bookshelves lined with colorful books, and the nautical-print cushions on the window seats. They didn't look like tourists; instead of shorts and T-shirts, they wore slacks and expensive-looking button-down shirts, and had a decidedly businessy air to them. I'm not sure why, but something about the way they were looking at the store's interior made my radar go off.

There were a couple of other browsers in the store.

"Can I help you?" I asked.

"We're just browsing," said the younger man. With their long noses and brown hair, the two men looked like they were stamped from the same mold, only with different hairlines. The older of the two stood back, hands in his pockets, as the younger man poked around.

"The business section is in the back," I said, guessing that that was more up their alley than the books we'd recently shelved on botany.

"Thanks," the younger of the two said shortly. "We're actually looking for a notebook; do you carry them?"

"Not yet," my daughter piped up, glancing at me. "But we should have some shortly; we're expanding our offerings."

"Unfortunately, that doesn't help us today," the man said. "Interesting little bookstore you have here. Kind of off the beaten path, isn't it?"

"Booklovers will go the extra mile," Caroline said. Again, what was up with her today? Not that I was complaining.

"Can I interest you in a particular genre?" I asked.

"No, no," they said. "We just needed some paper. Thought we'd stop by and check the place out. Mind if we browse?"

"Of course not," I said. "Let me know if you need any help."

He nodded, and the two of them retreated to the back room. I strolled after them on the pretense of checking on a book, curious to see what they were talking about.

"I think we should stick to the current format," the older man said as I pulled a paperback off the shelf and turned it over. "If it ain't broke, why fix it?"

"It's worth considering diversification," the younger one replied in a low voice. "And considering the location, there's no real competition. It'll certainly be more modern; that'll be a draw."

"I don't know about that," the older man said. "This isn't Boston... people are looking for a seaside experience. Take a look at the folks walking around... hip isn't what they're looking for."

"That's our brand," the younger one said. "We can stay true to the brand and make a nod to the area. And merch will help increase the profitability."

"It's worth considering," the other man said. "They're cutting us a good deal, I'll say that."

"Do you think the customer base will transfer? How much local pride is there?"

"Most of them aren't local. And we'll be recognizable."

As he spoke, the door opened, and Denise walked in with two willow baskets, followed by Bethany, who was carrying a box that was likely the day's shipment of books. Denise was still wearing her Sea Beans T-shirt.

"Hi, guys!" I greeted them. "New books?" I asked Bethany.

"Yup. I'll get them into inventory and shelve them," she answered briskly.

"Thanks," I said with a smile. What would I do without Bethany?

Denise shifted the baskets from one arm to the other. "You ready?" she asked as I shelved a copy of Bernd Heinrich's *A Year in the Maine Woods* in the Local Interest section. As she spoke, she spotted the men in the back of the store, and her face turned stony. "What are they doing here?" she asked.

"Browsing," I told Denise. "They were looking for paper."

In the meantime, the men were talking in the back. "I think it should be profitable, since we're the only game in town," one of the men said.

"It's a local coffee shop," my friend said loudly, and I looked at her, puzzled. "It should stay that way. It's not right."

The younger man looked at her, a bemused smile on his pale face. "Ah. You must be the manager who was hoping to take the reins. There might be a job for you, if you play your cards right. We could use someone with local connections."

"I wouldn't work for you if you were the only employer in town," she spat. "People like you shouldn't be allowed to come in and take over small towns. Sea Beans shouldn't be a chain," she said. "I can't believe you're trying to take it away from me."

"The contract will be signed tonight," he said, smirking. "Sea Beans will soon be the newest location of Epoch Coffee. Right, Dad?" he added, looking up to the older man beside him.

"That's the plan," the young man's father said, puffing his chest out. He reminded me of an overweight peacock, somehow, only wearing wingtips instead of actual wings. He brushed a bit of lint off his sleeve, as if it somehow represented my friend. "Charles Carsten. And this is my son, Chad. I'm sorry to hear you're disappointed, but we're not taking anything away from you. We're simply businessmen doing business."

"You're a thief," she said. "And I hope you get what's coming to you." She turned to me. "I'll be in the car."

"Let me just get my stuff," I said as she stormed out the door. Caroline and the other shoppers were all goggling at the man who had just declared he was buying Sea Beans. I glanced over at Bethany and Caroline. "You two have it under control?"

"Affirmative," Bethany said brightly, and Caroline nodded.

"Let me know if you have any trouble," I said, darting a glance at the men in the back room.

"We've got it under control," Bethany assured me, and then, in a quieter voice, said, "I can't believe Sea Beans is going away."

"Nothing's been signed yet," I said, trying to sound optimistic. "This is the first I've heard of it. I'll talk to Denise and find out what's going on."

"Let us know," my assistant said. "I'll do what I can to save the store, if it's possible." Ever since Bethany had discovered she might be in line to inherit a fortune (she'd discovered she was related to one of the island's old money families), she'd seemed more confident and optimistic. She'd been attending school part-time and working for me part-time to save money; if the funds came through, she'd be able to focus more on her studies—and her fledgling writing career.

She had hired an attorney my friend/maybe-more-than-friend Nicholas had recommended, and although it was early days, she was hoping she'd have enough to pay for her college education and maybe pay off her parents' house. As much as I wanted her to get an education, I'd be sad to lose her. Caroline was a little less motivated on the college front; I was hoping that spending time with my motivated assistant would encourage her to go back and finish her degree. I looked at the two young women tenderly. Caroline wore an oversized green Maine sweatshirt, freckles sprinkling the bridge of her nose and a few tendrils escaping from her long, reddish braid. Bethany, beside her, was in jeans and a tailored red sweater that set off her sparkling, long-lashed dark eyes and halo of black hair. They looked so different on the outside, but were both beautiful and full of promise. I knew both would find their way, but I hoped it would be as smooth as possible for them. Being a young woman could be tough. I knew that from experience.

But right now, I wasn't worried about Bethany or even Caroline. I was worried about Denise. I grabbed my purse and a jacket and headed for the door, looking back over my shoulder at the two young women behind the desk and hoping they'd be okay. Which was ridiculous, really, but I felt motherly toward both of them, even though only one was my biological daughter.

Denise was sitting in her Jeep with the engine on. I could practically see the steam rising from her head as I hobbled over and open the door.

"What's wrong with you?" she asked.

"I turned my ankle this morning." I raised a leg to show her the Ace bandage. "It's just a mild sprain."

"What did you do?"

"Slipped on a rock," I said.

"Are you sure you'll be okay?" she asked.

"I'm not going to miss out on blueberry picking because of a sore ankle," I said. "It's only a little strain. Besides, we need to catch up."

"Just be careful, okay?" she said. "I'll drive. You put your foot up on the dash or something."

I levered myself into the passenger seat as Denise tucked the baskets behind the seat.

"Tell me more about what just happened," I said as she

climbed in beside me. "Who are those people who say they're buying Sea Beans?"

"Out-of-towners," she said, with more than a hint of bitterness.

"I thought Margaret was selling it to you?"

"She was. Until Chad Carsten talked her into selling him the store so he can rebrand it as an Epoch franchise," she said.

"Doesn't Epoch do the organic paleo stuff down in Portland?"

"And everywhere else."

"Have you talked to Margaret about it?"

"I did, but she told me that unless I could match their offer, she wouldn't be able to accept it," she said, turning the key and hitting the gas hard. She put it into first gear and turned out of the parking place with a jerk that made me think that maybe I should have done the driving after all.

"Didn't she promise to sell it to you?" I asked, pulling my hair up into a bun to keep it from whipping around my face as she put the Jeep in second gear and gunned it. I quickly grabbed onto the top of the door to keep myself from being rocketed right out of the Jeep. "She said she'd sell it to you when the time came."

"That was before Chad came and offered her twice what I can pay."

3

"W hat?"

"Apparently values are up since Margaret and I talked," she said. "Snug Harbor's a hot market right now... business is good."

Except for my business, I thought. Were bookstores dead? Was it my location? Was I doing something wrong, or had I just overestimated the demand? I pushed the intrusive thoughts out of my head and returned my focus to my friend. "I thought you had a verbal agreement. You've been working toward saving up to take the store over for years!"

"She said it's business. She told me she'd recommend they keep me on as a manager. But Chad wants to totally change everything."

"So it won't even be Sea Beans anymore."

"Exactly," she said, looking miserable as she whipped us around a bend and gunned the Jeep past an old Cadillac. My hands were starting to cramp from holding onto the door so tightly.

"I can't believe she's willing to let the business be obliterated like that, after all the time she's put into it."

"Me neither," she said, and her jaw clenched briefly. "I feel betrayed."

"I would, too," I told her. All of a sudden, she hit the brakes; a moment later we were turning down a narrow paved road lined by tall, dark-green conifers. The temperature dropped, and when I inhaled, the air was perfumed with pine and balsam fir; despite the anger emanating from Denise, I could feel my body relax. We drove on for a while, past several dirt driveways that disappeared into the woods, before the trees gave way, revealing an open meadow I could tell even from a distance was loaded with the lime and deep green leaves of low bush blueberries. She pulled over onto the narrow dirt shoulder and, to my relief, turned off the Jeep.

"What should I do?" she asked, turning to me, her pretty face distraught.

"Talk to Margaret again," I suggested. "Write a letter about how much the store means to you, how special the place she created is, and how it would be a loss to Snug Harbor if it were taken over by a Portland chain. Can you raise what you're willing to offer?"

"I might be able to borrow more... I have to go to the bank. But I don't want to bankrupt myself."

"That makes sense," I said. My heart hurt for my friend... and for the potential loss of Snug Harbor's familiar coffee shop, which had been around as long as I could remember. "Do you have someone who could go in with you on it?" I suggested. "I've got all my money tied up in the bookstore, but surely there's some rich angel investor who doesn't want Sea Beans to go away?"

"That's an interesting idea," she said, her jaw relaxing slightly.

"Worth thinking about." My eyes drifted to the blueberry bushes. "Don't give up yet; you haven't exhausted all the avenues. And the other company can always change its mind!"

"Here's hoping," she said glumly.

"Let's get our baskets and get out to the bushes... and I want to run something by you. Something I heard this morning." I figured a change of topic might help distract her for a little bit.

"Is someone buying your store, too?" she asked bitterly as she opened the door of the Jeep, jumped out, and reached in the back for the baskets.

"No," I said as I got out and closed the Jeep door behind me. "But I think I heard two people planning a murder today on the shore path."

Denise stopped, a basket in each hand, and blinked at me. "You're kidding me."

"I wish I were," I said, and took one of the tightly woven baskets. As we walked to the blueberry barren, a stretch of slightly boggy ground that was covered in sweetfern, cranberries, small woody shrubs... and most importantly, little green bushes studded with tiny, plump blueberries, I told Denise what I'd heard that morning. "That's when I turned my ankle," I explained. "I was trying to see who it was and wasn't watching my footing."

"Have you told the police?"

"No," I said. "What am I going to tell them? That I heard two faceless people, one of whom has brown hair, discussing a murder on the shore path?"

"It isn't much to go on," she admitted. "Did you notice if either of them had an accent?"

"Nothing unusual," I said. "It was a man and a woman, though."

"Well, that narrows it down."

"I know, right?" I sighed. "I hate having this knowledge and not being able to do anything with it."

"I know the feeling," she said as she bent to pluck a bunch of plump dark berries, their skins dusky with bloom, and put them into her basket. I grabbed a small bunch too, but popped them into my mouth instead of the basket.

"Maybe I shouldn't have brought the basket," Denise said. We picked berries for a while, both caught up in our concerns, before my friend stood up, stretched, and said, "How are you and Nicholas, by the way? Any progress on that breakthrough?"

"You mean the code we figured out?" Seaside Cottage Books, it turned out, had once been owned by a rumrunner, and together, Nicholas and I had been investigating a journal and radio we'd discovered hidden in the stone walls.

"Yeah. Didn't it give you some locations?"

"It did," I said. "We've been to the first few, but haven't found anything. I'm afraid it may be a dead end, or just a list of rendezvous points."

"So you haven't found the ill-gotten gains he theoretically buried to hide from his wife?" The legendary rumrunner's wife, evidently, had not only been a teetotaler, but was completely unaware of her husband's clandestine activities.

"Not yet," I said. "It's probably just a local legend. But it's been a fun puzzle to try to solve; we're going to check out a few more this weekend."

"How are things going with Nicholas, anyway?"

"They seem fine," I said, blushing. "We're enjoying each other's company... but I think we're both being cautious. I know I am, anyway."

"It's weird dating after divorce, isn't it?"

"It is," I confirmed, nodding. "And Ted may have moved on quickly, but I'm still trying to find my sea legs." The ink had barely been dry on the divorce decree before he picked up his glamorous new girlfriend, discovering hidden depths in himself that I would have loved for him to have discovered while we were still married. We were still better apart than together, though, even though the adjustment to my new circumstances was still in progress. "I haven't lived on my own since college, and I want to see what I like and don't like when I'm the only person I have to think about," I mused as I picked a particularly big berry and popped it into my mouth. "Although with Caroline back, it's not quite like being alone."

"I thought she was staying with your mom?"

"She is, but she's at the store a lot. I'm happy about that, actually—it's good to see her—it's just that it's easy to fall back into that 'taking care of other people' role, and I'd like to find out what it's like when it's just me."

"That makes sense. Is she helpful at the store?"

"She is... she and Bethany are getting along, and she was full of ideas to promote the shop earlier today. I'm afraid she's not going to go back to college. I just wish she had some sense of direction in her life, you know?"

"Maybe running her own business might be something she's interested in," Denise said as she plucked a few more berries and put them into her basket. My own basket wasn't filling very fast; I seemed to be putting as many berries into my mouth as I was saving, although who could blame me? Was there anything better than fresh-picked Maine blueberries on a breezy summer day? "Although you should probably warn her about sharklike investors. It's a good thing you bought the store when you did."

"I'm worried about that actually," I confessed as I combed another plant with my fingers, filling my cupped hand with berries I dropped into my basket. "Receipts haven't been what I'd hoped. I'm a little far away from the main drag; apparently the shop next door closed from lack of business. I need to find some way to get people into to the store and spending money."

"The cookies aren't working?" she asked.

"They help," I said, "particularly with repeat business, I think, but I need to do more." I sighed. "Caroline's putting together a Facebook page for the shop. Maybe that will drum up some more customers."

"You're trying to keep your business going and I'm just trying to come up with enough cash to outbid out-of-town investors," Denise said glumly as we moved to a new part of the barren. "This 'living the dream' thing is hard sometimes, isn't it?"

"It's not without its challenges," I said. "But neither of us are quitters."

"That's true," she said. "And at least nobody's plotting to murder us," she added, referring to the conversation I'd overheard earlier.

"That we know of," I replied. "Do you think I should tell the police?"

She shrugged. "It's not much to go on, but it couldn't hurt. We can stop by when we get back to town."

"And then we make jam?"

"Or pie. Or Blueberry Boy Bait," she said, glancing at my basket, the bottom of which was not yet quite covered.

"Blueberry Boy Bait?"

"You've never had Blueberry Boy Bait? We're making some," she declared. "Bring Nicholas a few slices and he'll be eating out of your hand. Assuming we have enough to work with, that is," she grinned.

"What is it?"

"I'd say coffee cake, but it kind of transcends coffee

4

*I*t was a wonderful few hours, and we finished with blueberry-stained hands (and teeth) and enough berries to make not only pie, but the mysterious Blueberry Boy Bait. I'd all but forgotten the body-disposal talk of the morning... and Denise hadn't mentioned Sea Beans since we really got started.

Once we rolled into Snug Harbor's quaint downtown, though, the cloud returned. As she drove the jeep past Sea Beans, we both spotted the younger of the two men from the bookstore... Chad. He was leaning back in one of the chairs outside the coffee shop, arms crossed behind his head, looking as if he'd already signed the contract and taken ownership. Across from him was Margaret Keen, the shop's owner and Denise's boss and mentor of several years.

"I still can't believe she's selling out like this. I want to go talk to them right now."

"Probably not a terrific plan, but I understand the impulse."

"She just told me it was an offer she couldn't refuse," Denise said. "Enough for her to retire on comfortably. Like I said, it was twice what we'd talked about; there's no way I can compete."

"Maybe it'll fall through?" I suggested halfheartedly.

She sighed. "I doubt it. Did you see him? He looks like he already owns the place."

She wasn't wrong. We drove the rest of the way to the bookstore in silence. As the little house with its cheerful roses came into view, once again I was struck by a sense of deep gratitude that Seaside Cottage Books was mine. Even if the roses could use a trim... and there wasn't exactly a stream of customers beating a path to my door up the curved flagstone walkway.

"Are you going to come in and make that magical coffee cake you were telling me about?"

"I've got a few things to do," she said, "but I'll text you the link to the recipe."

"Thanks," I said, grabbing my basket from the back of the Jeep. "I'll save you a couple of pieces. Want to come over for dinner tonight?"

"I can't tonight," she said, "but soon?"

"Of course," I said. "Let me know." I paused with my hand on the door. "You're not going back to Sea Beans now, are you?"

"I'm thinking about it," she said.

I sighed. "Just take care of yourself, okay? And thank you so much for taking me berry picking. It was great."

"Anytime," she said as I closed the door. She reversed out of the spot behind the cottage and headed up the driveway. I couldn't help but notice that she turned left, toward town, and sighed as I carried my half-full basket into the shop.

"How did it go?' Caroline asked as I shut the door

behind me. Her hair was pulled back in a high ponytail and she was perched behind the desk with her laptop open.

"I got enough for something called Blueberry Boy Bait, apparently... Denise is going to send me the recipe."

"Maybe we should give some to Bethany," Caroline said in a low voice, her eyes sliding toward the back room, where Bethany was standing with a young man I recognized from the library. It was Devin Mattola, the young man who had recently joined her writing group, and from the way the two were looking at each other, I got the feeling Boy Bait wasn't going to be necessary.

"Good for her," I said; Devin seemed to be good boyfriend material. And they both loved books. Thing seemed to be turning around for my young friend, I thought with satisfaction.

Now, if only my daughter could find her way.

SIRENS WOKE ME THAT NIGHT, wailing as they sped past Seaside Cottage Books and up the road away from Snug Harbor. A crack of thunder sounded as they faded into the distance, and I shivered. Had a lightning bolt started a fire? I hoped not... it had been dry lately, and the last thing we needed was a forest fire.

I was just drifting back off to sleep when the phone rang; it was Denise.

"What's going on?" I asked, sitting up straight. "Are you okay?"

"I am," she said, "but there are about six emergency vehicles up at the big house across the road from me."

I rubbed my eyes and pulled the phone away from my ear, looking at the display before holding it back up to my head. "It's two in the morning. Do we know someone who lives there?"

"We do," she said. "It's that Charles Carsten."

"The guy who's buying Sea Beans with his son?"

"That's the one."

"Maybe he had a heart attack or something?" I suggested. "I'm sure we'll find out all about it in the morning."

"I'm walking over to find out what happened," she said.

"Denise, the last thing they need is you sticking your nose into things," I warned her.

"I have to know," she said. "Otherwise I won't sleep."

I sighed. "I can't stop you, but I still think it's a bad idea."

"I'll think about it," she said.

"Just go to bed and you'll hear all about it at the coffee shop in the morning. And then you can call me and fill me in." Winston looked up at me, his soulful eyes gleaming in the faint light streaming through the window, and sank his head back down on the blanket beside me.

"All right," she said. "But I have a funny feeling about this."

"Go to bed, Denise," I repeated, and hung the phone up a moment later, just as another peal of thunder sounded and the first drops of rain hit the window pane.

I HAD BARELY DRAGGED myself to the kitchen and started the coffee the next morning when the phone rang again. It was Denise. I checked the time: it was just after eight.

"So what's the story?" I asked, cradling the phone between my shoulder and my cheek as I measured the second scoop of coffee and poured it into the filter.

"He's dead," she said. "His big convertible Bonneville

rolled right off the cliff onto the rocks with him in it. I saw suitcases on the rocks."

"What do you mean, you saw suitcases on the rocks? I thought you were going to bed?"

"I couldn't sleep," she said. "So I went up the driveway and walked through the trees and looked at where they were directing the searchlights. The car's still down there, but they had to lift him out with a helicopter."

"So you know he's... gone?" I asked.

"I called the hospital to see if he had been admitted. They had no record of him."

I sighed. "You should have been a reporter," I told her. "So if he is gone, do you think Chad is still going to buy Sea Beans?"

"I hope not," she said. "I got the impression Charles was the money man." She sighed. "I do feel kind of bad about it, but then again, Margaret has been promising to sell it to me for years. Maybe this was the universe's way of putting things right?"

I hadn't realized how much the looming loss of Sea Beans had affected my friend; I'd never heard her like this before. "We'll see," I said cautiously. "Even if he is gone, Chad is likely in line to inherit. And even if not, Epoch might partner with someone else, or Margaret might decide she can get more for the shop. Don't count your chickens..."

"I know," she said. "I just... it was so upsetting to see my life plan just kind of whisked away from me like that."

I knew a little bit about what she was talking about. Getting divorced was a lot like that; I was still adjusting to my new reality.

"Are you working today?" I asked.

"I have the afternoon shift. I'm hoping I can talk to Margaret."

"I'd wait until it's official and you know what's going on," I advised. "Give her a day or two to process."

"You're probably right," she said. "You always give such good advice."

"And you always do such a good job of following it," I said dryly. "I still can't believe you went up there!"

"Maybe you're right," she said. "Maybe I should have been a journalist." We signed off a moment later, and I threw on some clothes as the coffee brewed. Once I'd taken Winston down for his morning potty break--the grass was dewy with rain, and the moisture made the smell of the beach roses even stronger than usual—I sat down on my little back porch with the view of Snug Island and pulled out my phone. I went to Facebook and typed Seaside Cottage Books, curious to see if we'd gotten any followers since Caroline put up the site.

So far, unfortunately, we still had three: me, Bethany, and Caroline. The picture on the cover photo was adorable, though, capturing the sweet little cottage with its front porch and gleaming windows, the front door open wide revealing a peek of the books within. She'd even found a little illustration of a cottage by the sea as our "profile picture." The content, however, was limited to her first post: Welcome to Seaside Cottage Books! Watch this space!

We were going to have to come up with more than that, I was afraid.

I was taking a sip of coffee when the phone in my hand buzzed; it was Nicholas. I instinctively ran my hand through my hair before answering in a voice that I hoped wasn't a croak; it was still early, at least for me.

"Good morning, Sunshine," he said. "I'm taking the afternoon off, so I was calling to see if you're free early this evening for some treasure hunting and then dinner."

"I'd love that," I said. Although the first three sites we'd visited since cracking the coded journal we'd found hidden in the store's basement had turned out to be a disappointment, it was still fun tracking down the sites on the map and imagining the clandestine activities that must have occurred at each one so many years ago. We'd found some broken glass and a few empty bottles, but nothing of any real value. Still, it was always fun spending time with Nicholas. I was starting to let my guard down a little bit again, learning to relax after several years of coexisting in a strained marriage. It was still strange being romantic with someone other than my husband; every once in a while I had to look down at my left hand and remind myself I wasn't married anymore. "Let me check with Caroline and see if she's free to cover the store."

"How's that going, anyway?"

"Better than expected, actually. She's got some ideas about making the business better; for the first time since the divorce, we're talking about something other than the divorce, and I'm actually seeing some enthusiasm."

"Good," he said.

"The downside is, I can't really afford her salary and sales are running about twenty percent off what I projected," I said.

"Not so good."

"Exactly. I'm hoping some of her marketing ideas can really help out. I worry about the store next to me. If it were more of a draw, maybe some of the traffic would spill over to me."

"I can see that. Make your area a destination. It's a pretty little place with a nice back deck facing the water."

"Just like Seaside Cottage Books. It used to be a house."

"Maybe someone will turn it back into one," he

suggested. "But in the meantime, let's forget all about that and focus on treasure-hunting. After all, if we find old Satterthwaite's treasure, you won't have to worry about book sales!"

"Wouldn't that be nice?"

"I'll pick you up at four!"

AT FOUR O'CLOCK, true to his word, Nicholas showed up at the store. I waved to Bethany and headed out.

"Where are we going, anyway?" I asked as I climbed into the car next to him.

"Sutton's Island," he said. "At least according to my GPS."

"And how many more of these map locations are there to check out?"

"I'm not sure, but there are a lot," he said. "At least from my count. I've picked the most commonly listed ones first, but that might not be the best plan."

"They could just be drop-off and pick-up points," I agreed. "Probably not hiding spots."

"Well, if nothing else, at least it's a nice day to be out on the boat," he said.

He wasn't wrong. Thirty minutes later, we were heading out from the dock, Nicholas's little motor boat cutting across the dark blue water. We passed a few moon jellies, and I spotted a seal head popping out of the water, its owner checking us out.

I snuggled into Nicholas as he turned right after leaving the main dock. The air grew colder as we left the mainland, and the boat bumped as Nicholas steered it over the waves. I was glad I wasn't prone to seasickness.

About twenty minutes later, we approached a small

island with a few houses dotting the coast and a long dock that protruded into the water. Nicholas checked his GPS.

"It looks like a spot right next to the dock is our destination," he said.

"So probably a pick-up point."

"Let's check it out anyway," he said. We tied up a few minutes later and hopped onto the dock, then followed the directions on Nicholas's GPS app up a slight rise away from the dock to what turned out to be a flat granite rock.

"Probably no buried treasure here," I said. "Unless they managed to drag a boulder onto it and fill in around it."

"What are you folks looking for?" asked an old man who was rolling down the one cracked road on an old bicycle.

"Oh, we're trying to track an old rumrunner's locations," Nicholas said. "Looks like this was a dead end."

"There used to be a shack here," he said. "This land belonged to the original Suttons; they had their main house up there, but it's gone now," he said, pointing up a rise to a bare spot with a few young trees sprouting. "Was a carriage house or storage shed, I'm not sure which, but it was definitely here. You can see the iron bolts where they lashed it down," he said, pointing to a rusty nub in the grass.

"What did he keep in the shed?" Nicholas asked.

"Rumor has it some of the folks from the mainland stored hooch there... so you're not on the wrong track after all." His eyes twinkled. "Probably no treasure, though, if that's what you're looking for."

Nicholas grinned at him. "How did you know?"

"People have been searching for his hoard for almost a hundred years now. Nobody's found it, but we've had a half a dozen folks come looking over the years, hoping they can find the X that marks the spot. There's been talk of a map, but nobody's found it."

"I own the house Loretta Satterthwaite used to live in." It was her ancestor, Josiah Satterthwaite, who was the fabled rumrunner of Snug Harbor.

"You run Seaside Cottage Books now!" the man said. "You sold me an Edgar Allen Poe anthology a few months back."

"I recognize you now!"

"Edgar," he said, holding out a wrinkled hand.

"I'm Max," I said. "And this is Nicholas."

"Good to meet you," he said. "I'd invite you to tea, but I'm on my way to the weekly poker game. If you ever want to stop in and talk books, I'm always here!"

"And stop by the shop anytime."

He lingered for a moment. "Making any more of those turtle pecan cookies?"

I laughed. "Call and let me know you're coming and I will," I said. As Edgar rode off to his poker game, Nicholas and I walked around for a few minutes more. The island was sleepy, almost deserted... a far cry from bustling Snug Harbor.

"Well, we didn't find anything, but at least we know we're on the right track," Nicholas said.

"Not if everything in the book is just a rendezvous point," I replied. "But still, it's worth continuing to explore."

WE WERE JUST GETTING BACK into Nicholas's skiff when my phone rang. It was Denise.

"What's up?" I asked as I plunked down onto the bench of the little boat.

"They came to the store and asked to talk to me," she said.

"Who?"

"The police. They think I killed Charles Carsten."

5

"You're kidding me," I said to Denise as Nicholas looked at me, concern on his handsome face. "He was murdered?"

"I think someone must have done something to his car to make it go off the cliff like that."

A shiver passed through me. "That's horrible."

"I know," she agreed. "I thought it was just an accident... that maybe he had a drinking problem or something, and passed out at the wheel... but I got the impression they think someone messed with his car."

"But why you? You're not a mechanic."

"One of my ex-boyfriends is," she said. "We dated for six years, and he taught me a lot about cars... they've done enough research that they already know that. And someone told them about the Sea Beans thing, and how angry I was."

"That's not exactly a smoking gun. Of course you were angry."

"One of the neighbors saw me when I went over to see what happened."

"What was your neighbor doing up in the middle of the night?"

"It's still a small town," she said. "Everyone's nosy, and when there are police cars and ambulances involved, it's double. I'll bet it was that Jimmy Witlowski. He's got binoculars, and spends half his time spying on people with them. I heard he has a telescope in his living room so he can watch women getting in and out of their hot tubs on the yachts in the harbor."

"Nice," I said dryly. The sea breeze ruffled my hair, and the water lapped the sides of the skiff. Nicholas had a little furrow between his brows and was watching me intently. I held up a finger to let him know I'd fill him in a moment. "So they asked you a few questions. Maybe they're just doing due diligence," I said, trying to be optimistic.

"I don't think so," she said. "They told me not to leave town. And I heard the word warrant."

A chill went up my spine. That didn't sound good at all. "Where did this happen?"

"Sea Beans," she said, sounding miserable. "They came in and told me they wanted to ask a few questions. It was so embarrassing... and now, if Margaret thinks I killed Charles, there's no way she'll sell the place to me. Not that I could manage it from jail, anyway," she added in a morose tone.

"Let's not get ahead of ourselves," I said. "I'm sure there were lots of people who might have wished Charles harm. And maybe they'll decide it was just mechanical failure."

"Maybe," she said, not sounding convinced. "But could you ask Nicholas if he knows of a good criminal defense attorney? Just in case?"

"Of course," I said. "In fact, we're about to go get some dinner, but if you need to come over later on, I'm sure he'd be happy to talk with you." I looked over toward Nicholas, who was nodding his head yes.

"Are you sure?" she asked.

"Positive," I said.

"Thank you. You know, yesterday, I wouldn't have imagined things could get worse. But today..."

"I'm sure it will improve," I reassured her, hoping I was right.

"That doesn't sound good," Nicholas said as I ended the call and put my phone back in my pocket.

"It doesn't," I agreed, and filled him in on what had happened.

"So she threatened him in public and was seen near where he died last night."

"Pretty much," I said. "Plus, her ex is a mechanic, so she knows a bit about cars."

"That doesn't sound good at all," he said. "I wish I had more faith in the local police, but it's not exactly Scotland Yard."

That certainly had been my experience since moving to Snug Harbor.

"We should probably find out more about Charles Carsten," I said. "Like, who inherits?"

"And did he dump or cheat anyone recently?" Nicholas suggested.

"In the meantime, can you get Denise in touch with a good attorney?"

"I can, but the one I'm thinking of is not cheap. I'll see if she can cut her rates as a personal favor."

"Thank you," I said. "Dinner's on me."

"No way," he said. "You're trying to get your business off the ground. Once you start your own chain, then you can buy dinner. Save your shekels for your advertising campaign."

"Are you sure?" I asked.

"Positive," he said, and started up the skiff's motor. "Now, let's go grab us some lobster."

I smiled, watching the handsome man I had fallen for twenty-five years ago hit the throttle and turn us toward land. We might not have found old Josiah's mythical buried treasure, but I was feeling like I'd found a buried treasure of my own right now; one that was far more valuable than any money.

DINNER WAS MARVELOUS; I had the classic Maine dinner of lobster with drawn butter accompanied by clam chowder and corn, followed with a big slice of blueberry pie, topped off with a scoop of homemade vanilla ice cream. We were back at my apartment, sitting on my couch; Winston sat on Nicholas's lap while he scratched behind his ears, looking like he would be more than willing to go home with Nicholas instead of staying with me. I totally understood the sentiment.

"So," he said. "Things still going well with Caroline?"

"So far. It's the first spark of life I've seen in her since the divorce," I said. "But I want her to go to school. I'm worried that it's a decoy, in a way... something to do to avoid facing college."

"Has she taken any classes yet?" he asked.

"Nope. She was accepted to UConn, but she decided to defer. I think she doesn't believe she can hack it. Her sister is knocking her classes out of the park, so I don't think that helps."

"One of the downsides of being a twin, I suppose," he said, scratching Winston's belly as the little Bichon rolled onto his back and wriggled in ecstasy. "Maybe she'll find her groove in the store, though."

"I don't want her to limit herself."

"Do you feel you did?" he asked, cocking an eyebrow.

"I don't know," I said. "That's a tough question. Maybe I do. I always wanted to go to school and get a PhD in English, but then I got married, and then the girls came along, and then it was all about play dates and lunches and library trips... and I kind of lost sight of who I was, and what I wanted." I shifted on the sofa. "At the same time, though, I'm glad I had all that time with the girls."

"But it sounds like you lost yourself in there a little bit," he said gently.

"I think I did," I agreed. "And now that I'm no longer mother and wife, I'm starting to remember who I was all those long years ago."

He reached out to touch my hand. "You always did love books," he said. "You had your nose in one all the time when we were kids. So I think the bookstore is a solid step in the right direction."

"Maybe," I said. "If I can make the business work."

"Let Caroline help you," he suggested. "It'll give her a sense of purpose. And she might find she has a talent for marketing... maybe that would give her a direction in school. They have degrees in things like social media marketing these days, I believe."

"And maybe she could take some classes at the college here?" I said hopefully.

"Maybe," he agreed. "What's Bethany doing, by the way, now that she may have the money for school?"

"It's still tied up in the courts," I said. "She's here for a while, at least. I don't know what I'll do if she goes... she's my right-hand woman, for sure."

"Maybe Caroline can pick up some of the slack."

"Maybe you're right," I said. I was thankful she was living with my mom; as much as I loved my daughter, my apartment was barely big enough for Winston and me. With Caroline bunking on the couch, it had been way too crowded. "Thanks for talking through this with me," I said. "I'm not used to having someone to help me figure things out. I kind of got used to doing everything myself. It's nice having you in my corner."

"And it's nice having you in mine," he said, leaning toward me. A tingle coursed through me as I leaned back, and our lips had just met when someone pounded at the door.

WINSTON LEAPT OFF THE COUCH, barking at the top of his lungs, and Nicholas and I almost knocked heads together.

The moment was definitely gone.

I stood up and walked to the door, where Winston was standing, front paws on the door, barking his head off. I peeked through the curtain; it was Denise.

Winston stopped barking the moment I opened the door and threw himself at my friend, tail wagging. She bent down to pet him and then registered Nicholas on the couch. "I'm not interrupting, am I?" she asked.

"No," I lied, shooting Nicholas a sidelong glance. "Come on in. We were just talking about Bethany and Caroline."

"Everything okay?" she asked.

"They're doing great," I said. "I don't know how I'd run

this place without them. Come on in and sit down; I'll pull over a chair from the table and you can sit on the couch."

'As long as I'm not intruding..."

"Of course not." I waved the thought away. "Can I get you a drink?"

"I hate to ask, but if you have a beer... I could use something to calm my nerves."

"I've got Blueberry Ale in the fridge," I offered.

"I'll take it," she said, lowering herself into what had been my spot on the couch.

"Nicholas?" I asked.

"Make that two, if you've got them."

I pulled out three bottles and popped the caps, handing one of each to Nicholas and Denise, then slid a kitchen chair over and sat down with them.

My friend slugged back about half a bottle in one swig and let out a sigh. "That's better," she said. "Thanks for letting me come over. My nerves are fried."

"I'll bet," I said.

"I looked into Charles Carsten today," Denise said. "Obviously someone must have wanted him dead, so I figured I'd see if I could work out who."

"What did you find out?" Nicholas asked.

"Not a lot, strangely," she said. "He doesn't have much of an internet presence. Just a LinkedIn account."

"That is kind of weird," I said.

"What did come up?" Nicholas asked.

"He owns a company that runs three Epoch Coffee locations," she said.

"So maybe Charles was buying the store, and not Chad, after all," I said.

"Looks that way, although you'd never know it to hear Chad talk. Anyway, like I said, he's got three stores; the one in Snug Harbor is going to be the fourth. Or was going to be the fourth. Other than that... nothing."

"Nothing?"

"Nothing on LinkedIn, other than that he owns this company. And no address beyond the one in Snug Harbor."

"How long has he lived there?"

"Two years," she said. "That's when he shows up as owning Venture Investments, too. Before that, he just doesn't seem to exist."

"That is odd," Nicholas said.

"He must have money from somewhere," I commented. "Waterfront property, even if it is on a cliff, doesn't come cheap."

"And that antique Bonneville can't have been cheap, either," Denise said, taking another swig of her beer.

"Does he belong to any car clubs?" I asked.

"I don't know, but that might be a good place to start."

"There's an antique car meet up every Saturday morning," Nicholas said. "Right by the Town Green. It might be a good place to start asking questions."

"That's tomorrow," I said. "What time?"

"It runs from eight to ten. We could go together," Nicholas suggested.

"That sounds great," Denise said, even though Nicholas had been looking at me when he mentioned it. "Shall we meet there at eight on the dot?"

"Sure," I replied. "I have to leave by 9:30 or so to get the store ready to open, though."

"That should be enough time," Denise said. "And then Nicholas and I can go have breakfast."

I cocked an eyebrow at Nicholas, who said, "I may come keep Max company and help her open the store. We can pick up some pastries at Sea Beans, though."

"Sea Beans," she said grumpily. "I wish I was done with the place."

"You could always open a competing coffee shop," I suggested. I have no idea where the idea came from.

"Open a new store? How would I do that?"

"Rent a space, come up with a name, get some tables and equipment... you could create your own coffee shop," I suggested.

"But where?" she asked.

"Wherever you want," I suggested. "The store next door is up for lease. Why don't you call and see how much it would be to rent it?"

"Do they have a kitchen?"

"I don't remember seeing one—it was a T-shirt store most recently—but it used to be a house, so there must at least be some kitchen space. If not, I'm sure you could talk with a bank and figure out how to put one in."

"But we're so far off the main drag," she said.

I couldn't argue with that; it had been a problem for me, too.

"It doesn't have to be next door," Nicholas said. "It's certainly worth thinking about. Max was an assistant manager for years, and now she's her own boss."

"Assuming I can get sales up," I reminded him.

"Caroline's helping you with that," he said reassuringly. "I'm sure it'll all come together. You're still working things out."

"Thanks," I said, thinking I'd better work things out fast, or Caroline wouldn't be the only one moving in with my mother. I took another swig of my Blueberry Ale and sighed.

It hadn't been the best of weeks.

∽

THE NEXT MORNING dawned cool and clear, and white clouds dotted the bright blue sky as Winston and I headed out the front door the next morning bright and early, on our way to the Town Green.

It was only a few blocks, and it was a lovely walk. We'd had a light rain the night before, and this morning everything smelled fresh and clean, the faint scent of spruce and balsam mingling with the salt air whisking off the water. I had finished my first cup of coffee for the day, but my mouth was watering for a muffin from Sea Beans; although Denise had sent me her Blueberry Boy Bait recipe, I hadn't had a chance to try it out yet.

As I walked up Main Street, I caught an enticing whiff of coffee and something like cinnamon rolls. My stomach growled, oblivious to my budget, and I found myself drawn as if by an invisible string to the short line outside Sea Beans.

I tied Winston up to the bench outside and asked him to be good. He stretched out on the pavers, enjoying the sun on his fur, as I stepped inside the sweet-scented store.

Margaret, the owner, was behind the counter this morning, looking surly. Her dark hair was scraped back into a ponytail, and she wore a Sea Beans T-shirt that looked like it might be older than my daughters. Her skin was creased from years of sun exposure, but evidently she wasn't as susceptible to her wares as I was; she was trim and lean, with the body of a runner. "Tall skim latte!" she barked to the young man behind the massive chrome espresso machine.

"Yes ma'am," he replied meekly as she finished with the customer—a woman about my age—and turned to the line. "Next," she spat out, as if she were a drill sergeant and we were her new recruits. I was guessing she'd taken the loss of

Charles—and the sale—pretty hard. But with Denise ready to buy her out, why was she so upset?

The thought irritated me enough I almost turned and left... and then I saw the plump blueberry muffins, their sugared tops sparkling in the case, and all will left me.

She might lack bedside manner, but Margaret was certainly efficient. "What can I get you?" she asked as my turn came up.

"Blueberry muffin and a latte," I said. "I heard the sale was scuttled; I'm sorry it fell through on you."

Something flickered in her eyes, and her jaw set a little more; I got the sense her guard had gone up. "That'll be seven dollars and fifty-one cents," she said. As I counted out my money and tucked a dollar into the tip jar, she studied me. "Who are you, again?" she asked gruffly.

"I'm Denise's friend, Max. I'm sure she'd be interested in buying the store from you."

"I don't sell to murderers," Margaret said flatly, then, to the barista, "Grande latte and a blueberry muffin."

6

"*D*enise isn't a murderer," I said.

"The police don't seem to agree with you. I'd have been willing to consider selling to her, but I like fair play."

"Fair play? You promised her the store years ago," I flared, "and then decided to sell it to some out-of-towner and go back on your verbal deal."

"It's business," she said coldly. "She had the opportunity to meet the offer. She didn't. I have myself to look after, you know. I don't have a rich husband to support me."

"I don't, either," I said. "I'm a divorced business owner myself. And I would never treat someone the way you treated Denise."

"I have a business to run. I don't have time for this. Next!" she called, looking at the woman behind me in line, whose eyes were as big as the enormous glasses she wore.

I stepped aside, waiting for my drink, which the barista delivered to me a few minutes later along with a bagged blueberry muffin and an apologetic look. "Are you going to be here for a few minutes?" he whispered. "I need to tell you something; I have break in ten."

"I'll be outside on the bench," I said.

"Sugar is on the bar by the door," he said loudly; Margaret had finished with the next customer and was staring at us, eyes narrowed.

"Thank you," I said, and walked over to the bar, where I picked up two packs of sugar, a coffee stirrer, and a napkin before heading outside to rescue Winston.

Although "rescue" might not be the right word, since he was being fawned over by two little girls who knew just the right spot behind his left ear. He barely noticed me until I sat down on the bench and opened the bag with the muffin in it, at which point he scrambled to his feet and fixed me with his big brown eyes.

"Just a little bit," I said, slipping him a small piece of the muffin edge and then doctoring my latte. As I sipped, I glanced back to make sure my spot wasn't in direct line of sight from the cash register. It was a few yards down from the store; if the barista was concerned, we could always move on to another bench.

I bit down into the blueberry muffin, savoring the crunch of sugar, the tang of the blueberry and the moist crumb, then washed it down with a swig of creamy latte. Margaret might not be the best at customer service, but she knew what she was doing in the kitchen.

I had finished the muffin and texted Nicholas that I might be running a few minutes late when the young barista popped out of the door, untying his apron with one hand and pulling a vape pen from his back pocket with another. He glanced back nervously at the shop. "Can we go down the street a little ways?"

"Sure," I said, picking up Winston's leash and tucking

the empty bag into a trash can. "I'm Max, by the way. I own Seaside Cottage Books."

"I know," he said. "I bought two books from you last week."

"I thought I recognized you," I said, studying his face; he was young, with wire-rimmed glasses and a hopeful, bright look in long-lashed brown eyes. "Two books on learning WordPress, right?"

"How did you remember?"

I shrugged. "I'm always curious about what books people pick. Thinking of switching careers?"

"Don't tell the boss, but I'm hoping to learn to do website design. I'm Brendan, by the way."

"Nice to meet you, Brendan... I'm Max. And once you do put out a shingle, please let me know. Apparently the store needs a website, and I have no idea where to start."

"Really?"

"Really," I said. "Anyway... what did you want to tell me?"

He glanced back at the shop. "The guy who was planning to buy the shop from her? The one who died?"

"Charles Carsten," I said. "What about him?"

"He was a real jerk. I heard him and his son talking to Margaret the other day; he said some things about Denise that I've never heard before and said his son had promised to double whatever she offered to make sure she didn't get the shop."

"What kind of things?" I asked.

"That she'd been arrested for a DUI a few years back. And that she had a history of fudging bank accounts to get loans she couldn't afford."

"How would he even know any of that information... assuming it's true? I've never heard anything about it."

"I don't know, but when the police came by today, she told them everything he'd told her about Denise. And now she's decided she'll never sell to her... in fact, she's thinking of firing her. Says she doesn't want a killer on the staff."

I groaned. "And she's telling the whole town?"

"Of course she is. Poisoning the well." He glanced back at the store again. "She used to be different. She slipped on a step last winter and got a concussion, and ever since then, she hasn't been quite the same."

"Traumatic brain injury?"

"I've heard it can affect your personality. Unfortunately, in this case, it doesn't seem to be for the better."

I sighed. "Anything else?"

"Oh, one thing. I heard the guy who died on the phone with someone the other day. He was kind of upset about something... said he'd never heard of anything called 'safest life,' and that whoever it was should stop calling."

"I wondered about that too. I don't know if it means anything, but I know you're friends with Denise and want to help her, so I thought you should know."

"Thanks," I said. "Denise really got the shaft, didn't she?"

"The younger Carsten guy really wanted to buy this business," Brendan said. "I don't know why, since he wasn't going to keep the name or anything. I mean, why not just open a new store and compete?"

"I don't know," I said. "It is kind of weird."

"I thought so too." He glanced down at his phone. "I'd better get back in there."

"How can I reach you?"

"I'll drop my card off by the bookstore later," he said. "I don't have them on me. Tell Denise I said hi!"

"I will," I said. "And thanks."

"No problem," he said, and scurried back to the store.

I reached down to pet Winston and took another sip of latte, then we headed over toward the village green to meet Nicholas and Denise, still thinking about what Brendan had told me... and how Denise was going to react when I shared the news with her.

THE TOWN GREEN was lined with classic cars in a rainbow of colors when I turned the corner a few minutes later. Aqua Cadillac convertibles, bright yellow vintage VW Beetles, a pumpkin-orange Corvette from what I was guessing was the 60s... and even what appeared to be an old hearse, painted dark purple with orange flames.

Denise and Nicholas were inspecting the license plate of the hearse, which read "DTHTOGO," when I walked up behind them.

"Interesting take on the station wagon," I said as Winston sniffed a wheel and began to cock a leg on a white-washed tire. "No, sweetie," I said, leading him to a nearby lamp post instead.

"It is, isn't it?" Nicholas said.

Denise wore jeans and an Acadia National Park T-shirt; her hair was pulled up in a ponytail, and from the dark circles under her eyes, I was guessing she hadn't slept. She bent down to pet Winston, who jumped up to lick her face, and then stood back up and glanced at my cup. "Still patronizing Sea Beans?"

"I wanted to see Margaret," I said. "She's not happy... but I did find out why she's refusing to sell to you."

"Because she thinks I'm a murderer," Denise said with a sigh.

"Maybe," I allowed. "But apparently Charles told her you had a DUI and falsified documents to get a loan."

She colored. "How did he find that out?"

"It's true?" I asked, blinking.

She sighed. "I had a bit of a drinking problem in my late twenties. I wasn't quite an alcoholic, but I hung out at bars in the evening because it was too lonely to be at home. I got stopped one night on my way home."

"And the falsifying documents?"

"I don't know about that," she said, but her eyes darted downward. I glanced at Nicholas; he'd seen it too, but I gave him a brief head shake not to pursue it.

"And then there's the whole double-your-offer thing."

"That... that..."

"I know," I said, touching her arm. Her face was flushed red, and her eyes were hard. "Let's see what we can find out about him while these people are here, okay?"

"Okay," she said, taking a deep breath and scanning the area.

"What kind of car did he drive?" Nicholas asked. He was looking handsome in a red T-shirt that clung to his pecs a little bit and a pair of faded jeans that fit him just right. I tried not to stare.

"A Pontiac Bonneville," she said.

"So let's start there," Nicholas suggested, pointing toward a car at the far end of the row.

"Good thinking," Denise said. "Start with a fellow Bonneville enthusiast. But what do we ask him?"

"If he knows Charles Carsten," I suggested. "And if so, did he see him recently, or know anything about his personal life."

"That seems a little direct," she said.

"We'll work it out. Say we talked with him the other day, and he told us about the car meetup."

Together, we meandered over to the aqua Bonneville convertible, which was gleaming in the Maine sunshine. To my surprise, the person leaning against the back of the car was not a man, but a woman in a leather jacket and bright white hair cut and gelled into spikes.

"Is this yours?" I asked her.

"You mean Petunia? One hundred percent," she said, patting the top of the car affectionately with one hand. Her nails were painted the same color as the car, I noticed with a smile, and she wore lipstick to match. "I restored her myself."

"Where did you learn to do that?" Denise asked.

"My dad ran an auto shop," she said. "I was always more interested in the garage than the kitchen, so he taught me everything he knew, and I picked up his obsession with classic cars."

"I picked up some of that from my ex," Denise said. "I get it."

"Are there a lot of Bonneville enthusiasts in the area?" Nicholas asked.

"There are a few," she said. "Well, one fewer today, unfortunately. And one fewer Bonneville."

"I heard about that," I said. "Awful... some local coffee shop mogul... he went over a cliff or something?"

"He owned a chain of coffee shops, yes," she said. "They must have done pretty well... that car was worth a mint. A few of us went to his house for dinner once, too... he had money from somewhere. Waterfront property isn't cheap up here. I got the impression he'd been in other businesses before the coffee thing, but he didn't seem to want to talk about it."

"That sounds like an interesting evening," I commented. "Was it just a dinner for car owners?'

"For Bonneville owners," she said. "There are only four of us in town, so we all know each other. Well, three, now," she said, her pink lipsticked mouth pulling down a bit. She reminded me a bit of Ann Richards, the former governor of Texas, right down to her slight southern accent. "I'm Max Sayers, by the way," I told her, proffering a hand. "I recently bought Seaside Cottage Books. These are my friend, Nicholas and Denise."

"Nice to meet you," she said, taking my hand and giving it a firm shake. "Kathy Dunst."

"Now I'm curious about what happened to Charles. Do you think maybe he was depressed or something, and drove himself off a cliff?"

She laughed. "He never seemed depressed to me. Rather full of himself, actually. Like he'd gotten away with something big, but wasn't going to tell you what. I didn't really know him that well, though. But he was big in the car community. I've never met such an enthusiast." As she spoke, a little girl came up and touched the shiny back bumper of the car. Kathy turned toward her, then bent down to ask if she liked cars.

Denise, Nicholas and I glanced at each other.

"Love your car, Kathy," I said. "Thanks for talking with us."

"Of course," she said, looking up at us as the little girl touched the bumper a second time. "Enjoy the day!"

As we walked away, Denise said, "Well, that wasn't very helpful. We learned squat."

"I'm curious about Carsten's business background," Nicholas said. "We should look into it and see if he had other associates in Snug Harbor. Maybe a deal went wrong?"

"Maybe," I said. "And I wonder if Chad's in line to inherit the estate?"

"I have a contact who can do a quick background check on both of the Carstens," Nicholas offered.

"That would be terrific," I said, taking another sip of my latte. "What do you two want to do now?"

Denise sighed. "I don't see any other Bonnevilles here. I made some Blueberry Boy Bait. Want to walk to my place for breakfast?"

I'd already had a giant blueberry muffin, but I've never been one to say no to baked goods. "Sounds great," I said, then looked at Nicholas with a grin. "We'll see if it works. As long as you don't switch allegiance to Denise!"

"I like Denise, but she's not you," he said, giving me a kiss. "But I'm happy to be a test subject," he said. "Let me just text my contact to get started on the background check and then I'm good to go!"

7

*B*y the time Nicholas, Winston and I walked back to Seaside Cottage Books, we were both full of Blueberry Boy Bait, which Nicholas had declared a winner.

"I'm going to have to get baking," I told him with a sly smile as we walked up onto the store's front porch. "Don't want to lose you to Denise."

"No chance," he said, giving me a look that sent a zing shooting right through me. He had just leaned in when my mother's voice sounded from behind me.

"There you are!" she said. "I hope I'm not interrupting," she added as Nicholas and I sprang apart.

I turned, my face coloring. My mother stood at the end of the porch, hand over her eyes to shade them from the sun. "Caroline is going to be in in a little bit, but I wanted to talk to you about her."

"I'll head out," Nicholas said with a rueful smile.

"Thanks for joining us this morning," I said. "Let's touch base later?"

"I'll let you know when I hear back from my contact," he

said. "And we still need to set up a time to check out the next place on our list."

"You two still going after that buried treasure?" my mother said.

"I'll call you later," I told him. He gave me an amused smile and ambled down the front walk as I turned to unlock the shop door and addressed my mother. "So what's up with Caroline?" I asked.

"She's a mess," my mother said. "It's like having you as a teenager again, only she's glued to her phone all the time, too."

"She's trying to get some social media going for the store," I told her as I opened the door and walked inside, relishing the scent of books and old wood floors and balsam and blueberry candles from the display in the souvenir section. Maybe we should add a few more non-book items, I thought.

"I don't think she's on her phone doing social media for the store," she said, then hesitated. "I wanted to tell you she invited Ted to come out for a few days."

My ex-husband was coming into town? "What? He's not staying with you, is he?"

"It's summer, and everything was booked. Caroline asked, and you know I can't resist her..."

"What about his girlfriend?"

"I think she'll be here the second night."

"Oh my God. Really, Mom? You agreed to this without checking with me?"

"I'm sorry, sweetheart. She just kind of sprang it on me. I didn't know what to say."

"The word 'no' leaps to mind," I told her sharply. "Are you really hosting my ex-husband's girlfriend at your house? You're not giving them my room, are you?"

"Of course not," she said, looking distinctly uncomfortable. "I was thinking that if you'd like to come to dinner..."

"With her?"

"No. Just the four of us. Like it used to be."

"We're divorced, Mom. It's not going to be like it used to be."

"You know." She shrugged. "You're still family."

I sighed. "I'll think about it," I said.

"I was thinking maybe the two of you could talk to Caroline," she said. "About her future. Maybe if she knew you two were a united front..."

"Mom, we're on it, okay?"

"Just trying to help," she said, picking a piece of lint off her impeccable linen blouse and looking through the books on the front display; we'd picked a series of natural history books focused on Maine and New England. She wore bright white Capri pants that she always managed to keep clean, and wedges that set off her summer coral toenails. I looked down at my own grubby nails. Manicures and pedicures were pretty low on the list right now.

"How's business?" she asked, picking up a field guide to local birds.

"It could be better," I said.

"You could ask Kirsten to come back," she suggested. "She brought quite a crowd in last time. I'll bet they'd do an article on her at the paper, too."

Kirsten, better known to the rest of the world as K.T. Anderson, was a bestselling novelist who my assistant Bethany had arranged to have sign books at our grand opening. Which was when I'd discovered that her boyfriend was none other than my ex-husband Ted—now Theodore, at least according to K.T. In addition to changing his first name, since meeting her he'd suddenly acquired an interest in travel, books, lectures, museums... pretty much all the things I begged him to try while we were still married. I hadn't asked if she'd managed to break him of his Sunday, Monday, Wednesday, Thursday, and Friday night football habit. I was afraid she'd tell me he now took art and wine tasting classes with her instead.

"You're ruminating," my mother remarked.

"You think?" I said. "I'll consider talking to her," I conceded. "But I'm not having dinner with her."

"Understood," she said. "It'll be just the four of us. It'll be fun!" she said.

"Fun" wasn't the word that leapt to mind, but I grudgingly agreed. How bad could it be? I thought.

Ha.

～

I HAD JUST FINISHED RINGING up the purchases of a family of tourists when the phone rang.

"They came to ask me questions again," Denise said. "At work."

"Oh, no."

"I had to leave my shift. And then they told me again not to leave town."

My heart squeezed. "Oh, Denise. I'm so sorry!"

"It was so embarrassing. Everyone's looking at me now like I'm a murderer."

"I'm doing some research on Charles Carsten right now," I said, pulling up Google on my computer and typing in his name. To my surprise, I got a hit on social media; I clicked on the link, and found a picture on a Bonnevile classic car club, with Charles cozying up to a young woman. "He may not be on Facebook, but a woman who looks like she must be his girlfriend is. Someone tagged her in a post and named him, too; apparently he belongs to a Bonneville classic car club that has a Facebook presence," I said.

"What's on her profile?"

"Let's see. Lots of car pictures, of course," I said; the woman's name was Amanda Duncan, and her cover photo featured her and Charles lounging against a red convertible that was older than I was. And, sadly, was probably at the bottom of the cliff next to his house.

"What's her name?"

"Amanda Duncan," I said. "She's pretty cute," I said. She had raven hair cut into a bob, and the kind of figure that indicated she had a regular Pilates habit and no more than a glancing acquaintance with carbohydrates. I gazed longingly at the cookies on the plate by the register and then steeled my resolve, instead focusing on the picture on my computer. Charles and Amanda looked so alive. And now one of them was gone.

I scrolled through the pictures and then went to the "about" section of Amanda's profile. She was in her forties, was a physician's assistant, and lived just outside of Snug Harbor. Several of her photos showed her with Charles; they dated back at least six months.

"What did you find?"

"His girlfriend, I think," I said.

"I'm looking her up, too," she said. "Amanda Duncan?"

"That's the one."

"Wait," she said. "Short, dark hair, right? I know her! She comes into the shop every morning. Double skinny venti latte."

"Can you try to talk to her?"

"I'll give it a shot tomorrow morning," she said. "Assuming she comes in after what happened... and assuming they let me come into work or I haven't been arrested."

"I'll see what else I can dig up," I said. "What's the address of his house, again?"

"It's right up the street from me, but I don't know the number. He lives on the rich side, by the water."

"Do you know when he bought the place?"

"Just a year or two ago," she said. "I remember the for sale sign going down."

"So he materialized in Snug Harbor relatively recently," I said. "I wonder where he was before that?"

"I don't know," she said. "Surely there's something online?"

"Not that I'm seeing," I said. "But I'll keep looking. I've got to run," I said, as a woman approached the register. "Call you later?"

"Of course," she said.

8

I arrived at my mother's house about ten minutes after six. I recognized Ted's SUV in the gravel driveway, snuggled in next to my daughter's car. I turned off the car, checked in the mirror to make sure I didn't have the remains of my lunch salad between my front teeth, and took a deep breath before opening the door.

"Maxine!" My mother met me at the front door, arms wide. "I'm so glad to see you."

"I see I'm last to the party," I said, walking in and stopping short at the sight of Ted—Theodore, now—and Kirsten "K.T." Anderson—snugged up on the love seat of my mother's living room.

I looked at my mother and raised my eyebrows, knowing she could read what I was thinking but not saying. In short, *What the h***?*

They surprised me, she telegraphed back with her own eyebrows, and I glanced over at Caroline, who was perched on the edge of a rocking chair, her arms folded tight over her chest, her mouth a tight moue of disapproval.

"Max!" Kirsten disengaged herself from my ex-husband

and crossed the hardwood floor to greet me. Before I could even think how to respond, she pulled me into a bony, floral hug. "So good to see you. I'm glad we're going to have some time to get to know each other!"

"I didn't realize you'd be here with Ted," I said.

"I surprised him," she said. "Theodore thought I had a meeting with my editor in New York, but it got postponed, so I decided to tag along."

I glanced at Ted—Theodore, I corrected myself—who had stood up and was pulling at the collar of his polo shirt and looking a little like he'd rather be just about anywhere but my mother's living room right about now. Which made me feel infinitesimally better. He had lost weight since we parted ways; his shirt no longer pulled tight at the belly, and there was now a bit of bicep visible under the hem of the sleeve. Kirsten had been good for him, it seemed; I knew he suffered from high blood pressure, and the weight loss must help. He gave me a weak smile and said, "Good to see you," as we engaged in an awkward hug. He still smelled the same, like Old Spice deodorant and Tide laundry detergent, and the familiarity was jarring.

So much had changed.

"Caroline," I said once I'd disengaged. She gave me a tight smile and a long-suffering nod, but didn't get up.

"Can I get everybody a drink?" my mother trilled.

"Yes," Ted and I said at the same time.

"Gin and tonic? I know you both like them."

"Actually," Kirsten said, "do you have cranberry juice and vodka by chance? I can whip up some Cape Cods... that's what we've been drinking lately."

"I'm not sure, but I might," my mother said. "I have to check." With that, she disappeared, leaving the four of us in uncomfortable silence.

"Well, then," Kirsten said brightly. "Here we all are."

"Well spotted," Caroline grunted, then unfolded her arms and pulled out her phone. Ted shifted uncomfortably, and I shot my daughter a warning look.

"How are things going in Snug Harbor, Caroline?" Kirsten plowed on. "I hear you're working at your mom's store."

"It's fine," my daughter said shortly, not looking up from her phone.

"What are you working on, Kirsten?" I asked, hoping to distract from my daughter's rude behavior.

"I'm about halfway through a new book, actually," she said, and Ted reached over to squeeze her hand encouragingly. Who was this man? I wondered as she continued on, "It's about a con woman who fleeces a bunch of big rollers in New York and then disappears, leaving her boyfriend for dead. Everyone's looking for her, and it's a matter of whether the cops can find her before the people she bilked get to her. Or her boyfriend's parents."

"That sounds... intriguing," I said, glancing at Ted. "Does he recover?"

"I haven't decided yet, but the plot usually works better if you have an actual dead body, so probably not."

Ted seemed remarkably unconcerned by this plot development. "Do they manage to find her?" I asked.

"I don't know yet," she said. "I'm only halfway through. I haven't figured out how they're going to track her down," she said, sucking on her lower lip for a moment, "but I'm sure Ted will help me come up with something. He's so creative."

A retching sound came from Caroline's direction, and again I shot her the laser glare.

"Speaking of dead bodies, did you hear about that investor who went off the cliff?" Kirsten asked.

"I did," I said. "Do you know anything about him?"

"I heard a bit of gossip in town this afternoon, actually," she said. "Theodore and I were having lattes at Sea Beans and someone suggested someone named Denise might be responsible."

"I don't think so," I said. "Who was talking?"

"It sounded like the man's son, actually. He said some woman had sworn to kill his dad for ruining her future." She cocked her head. "He didn't seem too broken up about the loss of his father. If I were an investigator, I'd take a closer look at him. See who was named in the will."

I leaned forward, feeling surprisingly glad that I was having this conversation. "What else do you know about Charles Carsten?" I asked.

"I know more now than I did this afternoon, I'll say that. I was curious, so I googled him when I got home. Not much out there, actually. It's like he just exploded out of the ether about two years ago." She bit her lip. "Makes me wonder if maybe he had a past he was leaving behind somewhere."

"Like what?" I asked.

"I don't know. A bad marriage. A business deal gone bad. Maybe he spent some time in jail and wanted a fresh start? He does like his cars, though. He's all over the forums."

"You really did research him," I said.

"I'm always looking for intriguing story ideas," she said, just as my mother arrived, carrying a jug of cranberry juice.

"I found this in the pantry. It expired two months ago, but it should be okay."

Kirsten let a slight frown slip out before reapplying her smile. "That'll be just fine," she said. "I'll come make them with you." She got up and bustled out in a hurry; for a moment, I felt a little bit sorry for her. It's got to be hard going to your boyfriend's ex-wife's house for dinner. Particularly when your boyfriend's sullen daughter and former mother-in-law were in attendance. How exactly had this come to pass?

"Caroline," I hissed when I was fairly certain Kirsten and my mother were out of earshot. "Be polite."

"Why?" she asked.

"It's not okay to be rude to a guest... or your dad's girl-friend," I said, looking to Ted for support. Unfortunately, there wasn't much coming from that quarter; my ex-husband was just sitting there looking dazed.

"I didn't invite her here," Caroline pointed out.

"It's not your house," I reminded her. "We're all guests here." Although I did have to wonder what on God's green earth my mother had been thinking.

"Fine," she said, then stood up shortly. "I'm not hungry. I'm going to my room."

"Caroline..."

"Tell her something made me sick to my stomach," she said as a parting shot, then stalked out of the room.

9

"We can't let her talk to Kirsten like that," I said to Ted. Before he could respond, Kirsten and my mother sailed back into the room with a tray full of cocktails.

"We made Cape Cods for everyone!" Kirsten said in a gay voice, then registered my daughter's absence. "Where's Caroline?"

"She wasn't feeling well," Ted said. "She went to lie down. Oooh, these look amazing," he said, taking a brightly colored cocktail from the bamboo tray Kirsten proffered. He took a big swig and smacked his lips approvingly as I took my own glass from the tray.

"I thought you didn't like cranberry juice," I couldn't help but mention.

"I still don't like it straight," he said. "But I can't resist a Cape Cod."

"Right," I said, and took a suspicious sip from the glass in my hand. It tasted like... cranberry juice.

"Delicious, isn't it?" Ted said.

"Mmm," I said, looking down at my glass. It might taste

like cranberry juice, but at least it had vodka in it. I took another big sip. It was going to be a long evening.

"So," Kirsten said. "How are things at the bookstore? I love what you've done with the place; it's so bright and cheerful!"

"I'm figuring it out as I go," I said, taking a big swig of my Cape Cod, which was already almost half gone. "Caroline's going to help me get my social media up and running."

"Oh, social media is *so* important," Kirsten said, leaning forward and giving me a view of her expansive cleavage. She had dressed in slacks and a blue silk top that accentuated her curvy figure, and her nails were long and pale pink. "Without social media, I'm not sure if I ever would have made the *New York Times* list. I've got a great assistant... maybe she can give you some pointers. I can give you her contact information."

"Thanks," I said with a polite smile. While I wasn't actively opposed to Kirsten, I wasn't up for a buddy-buddy relationship with my ex's new girlfriend, either. "I'm wondering if the strategy may be a little different for a local bookstore than an author," I suggested, taking a diplomatic tack.

She waved my thought away with a slender hand. "Oh, it's all about buzz. You'll have them lining up outside the doors soon enough."

"Just like they did at your reading," my mother piped up. "It was so nice of you to come, Kirsten. I know Maxine really appreciated you taking the time... I know you must be in such demand!" I glanced over at my mother, who was looking at Kirsten as if she were a triple layer chocolate cake and my mother had just spent six months on the Keto diet. Was she really fan-girling my ex-husband' girlfriend?

"I was happy to do it," Kirsten said. "I love connecting

with readers. And I'm happy to do another reading whenever you like!" she added, turning to me.

"How long are you and Ted in town for, anyway?" I asked, changing the subject.

"Theodore and I are just up for the weekend. I've got to meet with editors Tuesday, so I'm afraid it's back to the grindstone." She twinkled a smile at me. "And I suppose I probably should get around to killing someone!"

It was an interesting profession, mystery writing, I thought as I finished my Cape Cod. A timer went off in my mother's kitchen. "Who's ready for dinner?" she asked.

"I am," I said. "And how about another one of these Cape Cods while we're at it?"

"I told you there were amazing!" Ted beamed, putting a hand on the small of Kirsten's back and guiding her to the kitchen. I waited until they were both turned away to roll my eyes and tipped my glass up to get the last bits of vodka into my system.

"What was that woman doing there?" Caroline asked me as we pulled out of the long gravel driveway and headed back toward Seaside Cottage Books; I'd put her behind the wheel instead of me, since I'd been hitting the Cape Cods fairly hard. Caroline, on the other hand, had spent all of dinner in her room, then announced she was going to open the store tomorrow and needed to spend the night in my apartment above the shop. Although it was more than obvious to everyone present that she really just wanted to be out of any house that my ex-husband and his girlfriend might be spending the night in. I was guessing my mother hadn't put them in separate rooms.

"By that woman, I assume you mean Kirsten? I don't know," I said, honestly. "I think grandma likes having a famous author in the family."

"She's not in the family," Caroline bristled, clenching her hands on the steering wheel.

"Honey, I know it's weird, but she makes your dad happy. You don't have to fall in love with her, but it might make things smoother if you were able to be... well, polite."

"Polite?" she huffed. "I was totally polite."

"If you call refusing to speak and then not coming to dinner 'polite,' then I guess you're right," I said. "But I kind of got a different impression."

"Whatever. Why is she here, anyway?"

"I don't know," I said. "I guess your dad is trying to smooth things over and make us all a big happy family."

"Well, we're not," Caroline spat. "The family is gone."

Her words felt like a shot to the gut, and I took a long breath before I responded. "Your family is and always will be here. Just because your dad and I don't live in the same house anymore doesn't mean we're not still family. We love you and we're here for you. Always."

I reached out to touch her shoulder, but she flinched away, and she barely waited for the engine of the car to come to a stop before she yanked the door open and bolted up the stairs into my apartment.

I climbed out of the car, my limbs feeling heavy and sluggish, and stood for a long moment at the top of the path to the beach, smelling the scent of beach roses and feeling the salt air against my face, then turned and headed up the steps to the apartment, where Caroline had already locked herself into the bathroom.

Nobody tells you there will be days like these.

CAROLINE WAS a lump on the couch when I padded into the kitchen at eight the next morning. I made coffee, filled a travel mug, then took Winston down to the shore path for our morning constitutional. It was a misty gray morning. The tide was low, revealing a swath of glistening pebbles mixed with broken mussel shells and dotted here and there with bits of bladderwrack, and the mist was curling around the trees and rocks on Snug Island. It was a pensive, moody scene, which suited my frame of mind perfectly.

Despite the stresses of the past few days, I could feel myself relax as I breathed in the sea air and walked along the shore-hugging path. I passed the main pier, where the sightseeing boats and a few massive yachts bobbed in the water, then rounded the point toward the row of grand mansions whose back windows fronted the Gulf of Maine. A seagull dove and picked up a crab as I walked by the spot where I'd heard what sounded like a murder plot just a few days earlier. So much had happened since then it felt more like a month ago. The yard adjoining the shore path appeared to be empty this morning, though, so there was nothing to eavesdrop on. Besides, I thought as Winston sniffed at a rock, I had bigger fish to fry.

As Winston and I stopped to sniff a mound of beach roses, I thought about what Kirsten had said yesterday about Charles Carsten. Had he had a past he'd left behind? If he had, it must have been pretty financially rewarding if he owned a chain of coffee shops. I was curious about his son, too. And who was his girlfriend, Amanda, and did he have other friends or associates? Even after searching for him online, I knew almost nothing about him except that he had a son who was planning to buy Sea Beans, and loved classic cars.

Speaking of Sea Beans, I was almost out of coffee; without realizing it, I'd managed to finish off the contents of my travel mug. "Let's go see if we can say hi to Denise," I suggested to Winston, and instead of retracing our steps along the shore path, we turned and walked toward town.

Main Street was already humming with tourists out enjoying the clear, bright morning and pausing to admire the gifts available in the shop windows. Again, I found myself wishing the bookstore were a little closer to the main drag, and wondered how to draw folks down to visit. I pushed the thought of my own business aside as the coffee shop came into view; there were more pressing things to worry about than my bottom line at the moment.

Denise was at the register when I pushed through the door of Sea Beans. Her normal cheery demeanor was gone, though; her face was drawn, and she was taking orders like a robot. Still, I was happy to see her working. She needed something to take her mind off her troubles, although making coffee in the store she'd hoped for so long to be able to buy probably wasn't ideal. Particularly when the person who had recently coopted her future had died under suspicious circumstances.

I took my place in line, enjoying the scent of freshly roasted coffee mixed with something delicious that must have just come out of the oven. I suspected it might be the big, sugar-topped cranberry-walnut muffins on a cake stand next to the register.

I had made it up to third in line and Denise still hadn't noticed me. As I ogled the fresh muffins and tried to whip up some self-restraint, a brown-haired woman clutching a dachshund stepped up to the counter.

"What can I get for you?" Denise asked in a rote voice that was nothing like her normal cheery tone.

"Actually, is there someone else who can help me?" the woman said.

Denise blinked. "Why?"

"I heard what you did to that poor man," she sniffed, pulling her dachshund tighter to her chest, as if Denise might leap over the counter and steal the little dog. "I don't want a murderer making my coffee."

10

*D*enise's face paled, and a hush fell over the coffee shop. My friend regarded the sharp-nosed woman—who resembled her dachshund, I now realized, with a long torso and squat, skort-clad legs—and then gave her an icy smile. "I don't know what you've heard, but I promise you, I haven't killed anyone. At least not yet. But I'm the barista this morning, so if you want coffee, you'll have to take your chances."

"I..." The woman looked around as if trying to garner support, but everyone in the shop averted their eyes. "I guess it'll be all right. All I want is a double-shot mocha latte," she said. "Extra whipped cream."

"I'll be sure to hold the arsenic," Denise said dryly. "To go?"

The woman nodded.

"Name?"

"Andrea," she said, watching Denise intently as she made the coffee. The woman paid with a credit card—no tip, I couldn't help noticing—and scuttled off to a corner table, hugging her dog and looking embarrassed. "Andrea

Bates" said the receipt; I read the name before it got picked it up and tucked into the register. I wondered how she knew about what had happened. Then again, in a town like Snug Harbor, everyone knew everything.

"Hey," I said when it was my turn.

"Hey," Denise replied with a ghost of a smile.

"You handled that well," I said, putting my mug on the counter. "I'm impressed."

"I've had some practice already this morning, I'm afraid," she said, grimacing. "The usual?"

"Yup; just a cup of drip. Plus one of those muffins," I said. "That's what I'm smelling, right?"

"It is," she confirmed. As she refilled my cup and put a muffin in a bag for me, she said in a low voice, "I'm supposed to meet with Margaret this afternoon."

"What about?"

"I don't know," she said. "But I don't think it's good."

"Call me, okay? Or just come over to the store."

"We're meeting at three," she said, eyeing the next person in line, who was looking decidedly frowny.

"Call me after?" I prompted her again.

"Sure. If I make it that long."

I WAS STILL worried about Denise when I opened the store an hour later. I'd made a batch of chocolate chip cookies, and most of them had made them down to a plate near the register. Not next to the register; that was way too dangerous.

I had opened the windows, letting the sea breeze through the little store, and tried not to get too distracted by some of the latest arrivals. There was a new Ellery Adams book that looked intriguing, and a China Bayles mystery that I had been anticipating for months. K.T. Andersen's latest had arrived, as well, and I couldn't help but think about how strange it was to see my husband of twenty years with another woman... and about the challenge navigating our new family structure was proving to be. Caroline had still been sleeping on the couch when I'd gotten home, and I'd found myself tiptoeing around my own apartment, but had finally kicked her up off the couch and into the bathroom; after all, she had been supposed to open the store for me. I hoped Ted and Kirsten went back to Boston soon; a small one-bedroom wasn't big enough for both of us. Besides, what was Caroline going to say if Nicholas and I started spending more time together?

I had shelved two boxes of books and was still ruminating over Denise and Caroline when two women in Snug Harbor T-shirts and lighthouse-themed tote bags walked in.

"Thank heavens, a bookstore!" breathed the shorter of the two. "Where's the mystery section?"

"Right over there," I said, pointing toward the wall to the left of the front door. "Looking for anything in particular?"

"A good Maine mystery!" she pronounced, and I busied myself pointing her toward Lea Waite's excellent Antique Print series and suggesting a few others by local authors.

"Perfect," she said, starting to build a stack of books. "And you've got squishy armchairs, too. Do you serve coffee?" she asked as I took a sip from my travel mug.

"Unfortunately, no," I said. "But there's a free Mississippi Mud Bar with every purchase!"

"Free Mississippi Mud Bars? I think I just died and went to heaven," said the mystery reader's companion, who had loaded up on romance novels and a few natural history books.

"You want them now while you browse?" I asked.

"We should probably wait so we don't get frosting on the books," the mystery reader said. "But thanks!"

As I returned to my shelving, a young, dark-haired woman pushed through the door. She wore high heels and a short dress that clung to her fit form, and seemed uncomfortable, as if it was her first trip to a bookstore. She didn't take her sunglasses off, but something about her looked familiar. As she looked completely adrift, I walked over and asked if she needed anything.

Her eyes darted to the door, as if she were afraid of being watched, and she reached for a strand of dark hair and wound it around her fingers. "Ummm... do you have anything on wills?" she asked.

"That should be in the personal finance section," I said, leading her to the corner of the store I reserved for business, self-help and finance. "Anything in particular?"

"I just want to know how inheritance works," she said.

"Right. Here are a few options," I said, pointing her to a shelf filled with titles on probate and inheritance.

"Thanks," she said, glancing toward the door once more before reaching for a "Dummies" book on wills, inheritance and estate tax.

"Let me know if you need anything else," I said as she started leafing through the pages.

She made a distracted noise and focused on the page as I headed back to the cash register, where the two women were ready to check out with their stacks of books.

"Some good reads here," I said as I began scanning the books.

"I just adore this store," the mystery reader gushed. "I can't understand why you're not completely full!"

"She needs a cafe," the romance reader said sagely.

I laughed. "I'd love a cafe, but I don't even have enough room for all the books I'd like to stock." Besides which, I added silently, I was having a hard enough time managing a bookstore, and I had experience with that. How on earth would I run a restaurant, too?

"Well, if you had one, we'd be here for hours," the mystery reader said.

"I'll think about it," I said as I finished checking her out and handed her a Mississippi Mud Bar.

"Oh, this is heavenly," she groaned, biting into it as she stepped away from the desk with her bag of books. "You've got the cooking part down, for sure!"

I laughed as I rang up her friend, and a few minutes later, they were both headed back out to the street, still oohing and aahing over their mud bars.

As the door jangled shut behind them, the young woman in sunglasses approached the counter; something about the way she moved gave me the impression she was expecting a lion to jump out from behind the Nature and Environment shelf and pin her to the hardwood floor.

"Find what you needed?" I asked as she set two books on the shelf: one, the Dummies book I had showed her, and the other a book on contesting wills.

"I think so," she said, opening her wallet and fishing out two twenties. Which was unusual; most people younger than seventy paid with a card. I caught a glimpse of the name on her credit card as she closed her wallet: Amanda Duncan. Charles's girlfriend... or ex-girlfriend, now.

"Family issues?" I asked as I made change for her.

"Kind of," she said. "Men. They lie all the time, don't they?" She dabbed at her eyes under her sunglasses, and then said, "I'm so sorry. It's just... when will I learn not to believe them?"

"Someone betrayed you?" I asked as I handed her the bills.

She gave a bitter laugh. "You could say that. He convinced me to sell my house and leave my job and live the good life, told me everything would be taken care of... and then..." She swallowed. "Well, a lot of things happened. And then he died. And I just found out that all the things he promised me? He lied about those too. I'm so sorry," she said, looking around as if someone might be listening. "I shouldn't be talking about this. I don't even know you. And the only reason I'm buying books here is I'm afraid if someone sees what I've searched..." She put her hand to her mouth; her face was pale and tears streaked her cheeks beneath her glasses. "I'm sorry. I just can't stop talking today."

"Grief does that; don't worry." I smiled and said, "Mississippi Mud Bar? Chocolate helps everything... and you get one free with every purchase."

"Oh. No, no thank you," she said. "I... They look great, but I just can't eat right now."

"No worries. Want me to bag one for you?"

She shook her head.

"Got it. Would you like a receipt?"

"No," she said, and gave me a short, shy smile. "Thanks for being so kind."

"I hope things go your way," I said.

"Me too," she said, and scuttled to the door, clutching her purchase to her chest.

Amanda Duncan. Charles's girlfriend, at least until his car went over the cliff. She had seemed genuinely upset, and very vulnerable. Was she grieving his death? Or the money he evidently hadn't decided to leave her?

I walked over to my computer and typed in her name. A

LinkedIn account came up; apparently she'd been a social media sales rep in California until last year, which must have been the time that she took up with Charles. I went to her Facebook page next. Her profile picture showed her with a big smile and the Maine coast behind her, a man's arm around her shoulder, and her cover photo was of a bikini-clad Amanda on a wooden sailboat with a drink in her hand and the wind in her dark hair. She was stunning, with a smile to match. I clicked on the link to her background. According to Facebook, she'd gone to a Kansas State and her hometown was a small town in Kansas; with an upbringing like that, Charles's lifestyle must have been a dizzying change. It was no wonder she'd given everything up to follow him.

On the other hand, she obviously thought she was going to come into some money after Charles's death. What had changed? Had things not been as rosy recently? Had he been seeing someone else? Is that what she meant when she said he'd lied?

I closed up the laptop, still thinking of the young woman behind the sunglasses as I returned to shelving books. I had emptied the second box when the upstairs door banged open. A moment later, Winston came clicking down the stairs, wearing his customary doggie smile, followed by my daughter. I glanced at my watch; it was almost eleven. For all her talk of being here bright and early in the morning, she had certainly taken her time getting up.

"Hi, sweetheart," I said. "What's up?"

She rubbed her eyes, and for a moment, I saw her dad in her; he made the same gesture when he came downstairs for coffee. Then she yawned and said, "Is there anything for lunch?"

"I think there's turkey in the fridge and some bread left on the counter; you can make a sandwich."

"No roast beef?"

"You're welcome to go to the store. Hey, you didn't open like you said you would; can you work from two to close?"

"Bethany's going to be here too, right?"

"She should be here at noon," I said.

"Good," she said.

"How's the marketing campaign going?" I asked.

"Well... we're trying to figure out a thing to draw people here."

"What about the cookies? Have you posted the pictures you took of the Mississippi Mud Bars?"

"Oh yeah, I better get on that," she said. "Bethany's seeing if she can line up some more author events, too. But not Kirsten again."

"Would Bethany consider adding a few more members to the writing group?" I asked. The group, which Bethany had started not long ago, met in the back room of the shop, and we'd sold a few more 'how-to-write' books, but it wasn't as big a source of traffic as I wanted.

"Maybe we should do poetry slams. Kind of open mic?"

"Interesting idea," I said. "In the meantime, why don't you do a post featuring some of our new additions? There's a great new book on Maine nature-watching we just got ten copies of."

She sighed. "I'll do it this afternoon." So much for this new enthusiasm for marketing the bookstore.

"Hey," I said. "Are you doing okay?"

She shrugged. "My parents just divorced and I can't even stay in my own house because there's another woman living there. What do you think?"

As I stood trying to come up with something to say, she

trudged back up the stairs and slammed the door behind her.

I looked down at Winston. "Well, that went well, don't you think?"

He cocked his head and looked at me, and I reached down to rub his head. Thank goodness not all relationships were complicated.

11

I didn't hear or see any more sign of Caroline before Bethany arrived at 1:30, with her new beau in tow. Bethany seemed to glow when Devin was around, and he treated her like a queen.

"Hi, guys! Hey, Devin! How's the book-writing going?"

"We're both in the mushy middles of our stories," Bethany said, "but we're hoping to hash things out at the group this week."

"In the meantime," he said, "I'm trying to convince this young woman to get herself into school full-time."

"I still don't know whether I'll have the money to pay for it," she said. "Besides... I don't want to leave Snug Harbor right now." She gave him a shy smile. "Things are good."

"So take more classes locally and transfer the credit when you're ready," he suggested. "Even if you have to take on a little bit of debt, it's not that expensive, and I can help you with scholarship applications."

She sighed. "I know I should, but I feel like Max needs me here." From the way she'd looked at Devin, I had the distinct feeling I wasn't the only reason—or even the main reason—for her reluctance to decamp from Snug Harbor right now. Still, she had her future to take care of.

"You can do both," I said. "And as much as I love having you here, and as important as you are to the store and to me, I won't have you putting your own future on hold for us!"

"Exactly," Devin said. "Listen to Max, if you won't listen to me. You have to take care of yourself. It would be a waste of your fine mind for you not to go to school! And besides, I can help Max out."

"You have a full-time job at the library," I pointed out.

"Yes, but if Bethany is in school, I'm going to have a lot of free time to fill. And I do know my way around books!"

Since he was a librarian, I couldn't argue with him.

CAROLINE MADE an appearance just before two, her demeanor chilly—at least to me. I left her and Bethany to it and headed upstairs to make lunch, only to discover my daughter had eaten all the turkey.

I looked at the couch with the pile of unmade blankets and the dirty dishes on the counter and decided it was time to get out of the apartment. I had been in the mood for fried clams for a few days, so I decided to take myself to the Salty Dog.

I could have driven, but it was such a beautiful day I decided to walk to town along the shore path. The sun was bright in a clear blue sky, white fluffy clouds gathering on the horizon like sheep, and the water sparkled as it lapped the shore. The tide was high, coming almost up to the path in places, and the beach roses were in full bloom, their rich, winy scent perfuming the salt air as I passed. The fuchsia flowers were flanked by bright orange rose hips, and beneath them, I recognized a few three-leafed strawberry plants nestled in the grass.

The Snug Harbor Inn, a grand building built on a point near town, was just coming into view when my phone rang. My heart leapt when I saw who was calling; it was Nicholas.

"Hi!" I said, feeling as if the sunshine had just gotten fifty percent brighter. "How are you?"

"Missing you," he said, making me smile. "How's Denise doing?"

"Not great." I related what had happened at Sea Beans that morning. "She's talking with the owner this afternoon at three; I was on my way to the Salty Dog for a late lunch of fried clams. Care to join me?"

"I'd love to," he said, "but I've got a client meeting coming up. I was actually calling to see if you would be available for dinner?"

"That sounds great," I said. "Yes!"

"Shall I come pick you up?"

My instinctive response was "Yes," but I thought about Caroline's response to her dad's new girlfriend and decided it might be easier to meet him somewhere other than my place. "Actually, why don't I come to you this time?" I proposed.

"Sure!"

"It's a date," I said.

"Looking forward to it. Keep me posted on Denise... and enjoy your clams!"

~

IT WAS ALMOST HALF past two by the time I settled in at the long wooden bar at the Salty Dog and put in my order for a basket of fried clams, a Snug Harbor Ale, and a side salad (so I didn't feel quite as nutritionally bankrupt).

"Honey mustard on the salad?" asked Sylvia, the woman behind the bar. She and her husband, Jared, owned the Salty Dog together; it was a popular place for both locals and tourists.

"As usual," I said.

"That's what I figured. How's Denise holding up, by the way?" Denise was my frequent companion to the Salty Dog, and we'd gotten to know Sylvia. She was a frequent visitor to Seaside Cottage Books; she enjoyed true crime novels, and I was sure what had happened to Charles was firing her imagination.

"I'm sure you can imagine," I said. Sylvia had been convinced Jared might be a murderer some time back; both were very relieved when the true killer was found.

"Poor thing," Sylvia said as she filled a glass from the tap for me. "So Charles really went over the cliff in his car?"

"That's what I understand," I said. "Did you know him?"

"I've seen him in here a few times. He and his son are the jerks who are looking to buy out Margaret down at Sea Beans, I hear."

"Yes, that's right. What was your impression of him?" I asked.

She cut off the tap and set my ale down on a coaster in front of me. "He seemed like he was trying to prove something," she said. "Working hard to impress people. I guess maybe I got that feeling from the fancy classic car he liked to drive. But it was more than that." She shrugged. "He wasn't someone I would have wanted to spend much time with."

"Did he come in here with anyone else?" I asked.

She shook her head. "Just his son." She sighed. "Denise

has really had a rough go of it. I just hate all these corporate entities taking over the town. There's supposed to be yet another big new building going in down by the shorefront soon. There'll be nothing left by the time they're done."

"I guess the only constant is change," I said. "As long as I can still get my fried clams here, I'll be happy."

"And as long as you keep stocking the new releases in the True Crime section, I'll be happy, too."

"I'll do it as long as I can," I promised, although I didn't feel particularly sanguine about the whole making-a-living-as-a-bookstore-owner thing today. I probably shouldn't be spending money in a restaurant, either, but you can't live your whole life denying yourself.

"I'll go get that order in," she said, heading toward the kitchen. "Let me know if you need anything else!"

"Thanks, Sylvia." As I sipped my beer, I heard a voice I recognized from behind me. I glanced over my shoulder; it was Amanda, with a young man I hadn't seen before. They were leaning in toward each other, oblivious to the rest of the world.

"Are you talking to an attorney?" I heard the young man ask.

"I probably should," she said. "It wasn't an accident. Someone cut the brake lines of his car. What if they think I had something to do with it?"

"Did you?" he asked, point blank.

"What? You think I'd do something like that?"

"No, no, of course not," he said quickly. "I just... I worry about you, is all." I raised myself in my seat a little; I could see the couple reflected in the mirror behind the bar. Her hand was in his, and they were looking at each other intensely, unaware that I was watching them... and listening.

I thought about Amanda's upset over "lying men" earlier

that day, at the bookstore. Now that I saw this, it confused me. Had she actually been two-timing Charles, instead of (possibly) the other way around? Had he found out about her extracurricular activities and threatened to kick her out or change his will? Had she taken action by cutting his brake lines to protect herself?

And where had he been going in the middle of the night in Snug Harbor, anyway? The town closed down at around ten at the latest.

"What are you going to do now?" the young man asked, bringing me out of my thoughts and back to the bar.

"I don't know," she said. "I got a few books on contesting wills, but I don't know any lawyers. Not that I have anything to pay them with, anyway. I can't go back to the house. I just... everything is just falling apart." She stifled a sob, and he made a gentle hushing sound.

"It'll be okay, Amanda. I'll take care of you."

"How?" she said, her voice edged with bitterness.

"I don't know yet, but we'll find a way," he said, squeezing her hand.

She sighed. "I can't eat," she said, poking a fork at her tiny Caesar salad. "Let's get out of here. I need some air."

"I'll ask for the check," he said. A moment later, as Sylvia set a basket of luscious-looking fried clams in front of me, the young man behind me flagged down a waiter and paid their tab with a credit card. They lingered for a few minutes after he tucked his card into his wallet, then got up and walked to the entrance; he held the door open for her, then gave her shoulders a squeeze as they turned right and started walking down toward the waterfront.

When they were out of sight, I slid off my bar stool and hurried over to their table, glancing at the name on the check. John Stanton.

Back at my table, I chewed on the first clam, barely tasting it as I thought about all I'd heard. Who was this John Stanton?

And was Amanda responsible for what had happened to Charles?

I was replaying their conversation in my head when Sylvia came to check on me. "How are the clams?"

"As delicious as always," I said as I swallowed one of the golden-fried shellfish. "Hey... did you recognize the two young people sitting at the table behind me a few minutes ago?"

"Amanda Duncan? She's been in from time to time; we talked once or twice."

"Did she ever say anything about Charles?"

Sylvia cocked an eyebrow and leaned forward, eyes gleaming. "Do you think maybe she did it?"

"I'm just wondering," I said with a shrug.

"I'd be wondering pretty hard if I were you," she said. "I know you and Denise are close, and I didn't want to say earlier... but I'm worried she might be arrested soon."

"Where did you hear that?"

"It's all over town."

"What do you mean?" I asked, feeling like someone had dashed me with ice water. I knew a few customers had been rude at Sea Beans, but I had no idea the Snug Harbor court of opinion had convicted my friend so thoroughly.

Sylvia shrugged. "I heard she hung around to see it happen. You know her ex was a mechanic, right?"

"Denise had nothing to do with what happened to Charles," I said. "I know her. She's fiery, but she's a good and moral person. She would never hurt a fly."

"You and I know that," she said. "But there's actually a

precedence for her getting violent. She punched a guy in the face at Sea Beans last year."

"What?"

"I don't like to talk out of school," she said, a little embarrassed. "Ask her about it. I'm not sure if he pressed charges, but from what I heard, he could have."

"Again, I'm sure she had nothing to do with Charles," I said, trying not to sound defensive. "Do you know anything about him?"

"Not really, aside from the fact that I didn't like him much," she said. "He and his son came in to watch games from time to time," she said, glancing over her shoulder at the TV in the corner.

"Did they seem to get along?" I asked.

"They did," she said. "I only heard them argue once. Something about having to leave California."

"California?" I asked.

She nodded. "His son told him he'd been 'sloppy.' Charles turned bright red and told him his 'sloppy' business practices were what paid for his car, his college, his fancy clothes, and the rest of it. And that he hardly had a leg to stand on."

"What was he talking about?"

She shrugged. "I don't know, but that sure shut Junior down. His dad stormed out of the place, and Junior paid the bill and scuttled after him."

"When was this?"

"About a month ago," she said. "The Patriots game was on. It was much more exciting than the game itself; that was a low-scorer, as I recall."

"Huh. Have they been in here since?"

She looked up for a moment, considering. "Not that I can think of," she said. "I saw Junior in here a week ago or so, with a pretty young lady in a dress. She had a southern accent, and seemed completely into him. But I never saw Charles again." She wiped down the bar and rearranged a stack of menus. "It's a sad thing. Money can't protect you from everything, can it?"

"No," I said, eating a clam contemplatively and thinking about everything I had just learned. "It really can't, can it?"

MY BELLY full of clams and Snug Harbor Ale, I stepped out of the Salty Dog and into a bright, clear afternoon. I walked down the quaint, tree-lined street, glancing over at Sea Beans and wondering how things were going for Denise, although if my conversation with Sylvia was any indication, I had a feeling I already knew.

I headed down the main street a block, catching a whiff of balsam fir as I passed a gift shop and resisting the urge to get a double scoop of black raspberry ice cream on a waffle cone at Scoop's Ice Cream then turned down a leafy residential street I knew led back to the shore path. Within minutes, I had the Gulf of Maine at my feet, the deep blue water lapping at the shore, the emerald green trees on the outer islands sprouting up from granite bluffs, and seagulls wheeling overhead. A cool breeze riffled the waves and caressed my face, and I felt something inside me release a little bit. One of the things I treasured about Snug Harbor was the proximity of nature and the wild, rugged beauty of the coastline; I'd missed that living in Boston during the girls' childhood. Being here connected me to my own childhood, too, and the girl I had been before I took on the roles of wife, then mother. It was easy to forget who you'd been when you were ten and barefoot and scampering along the rocks looking for crabs, no worries but whether or not you'd have enough pocket money for a bit of fudge or ice cream and whether you'd find a shard of rare purple sea glass at low tide.

It was thirty years later, but I still got excited when I caught the gleam of sea glass among the mussel shells and bladderwrack, and the shock of the cold water on my toes never grew dull. I had all the worries of adulthood—my children, my foundering business, and not least the threat to my dear friend Denise—but just being here reconnected me to the girl I had been, with hopes and dreams and a wild streak that felt raw and true.

It was probably that reconnection that had spurred me to follow my old childhood dream of one day owning a bookstore of my own and buying Seaside Cottage Books. I reached down to pluck a piece of pale blue glass from beneath a rock, feeling a twinge of fear that that dream might soon come to an end.

I pushed that defeatist thought away. Worrying wouldn't help anything. I needed to dig down and find the grit and creativity to keep my dream alive... and keep my friend Denise out of jail.

12

*M*y phone rang just as I was strolling down the shore path, past the spot where I'd heard a suspicious conversation a few days earlier; it was Denise.

"How did it go?" I asked, sliding onto a bench tucked along the shore path against the back fence of one of the mansions that stood here. The wooden bench was flanked by rosebushes and had a sweeping view of the gulf and a smattering of off-shore islands, whose dark green trees contrasted with the sparkling blue water, and a cool breeze riffled my hair as I leaned back with the phone pressed to my ear.

"Margaret suspended me," my friend said, sobbing.

I sat up straight. "What? Why?"

"Too many customers complained about me; the whole town thinks I murdered Charles Carsten, apparently. She's afraid it will be bad for business." She choked back a sob. "Everything went south for me the moment that man stepped into Sea Beans. My whole future, which I've been working toward for years, has evaporated. Instead of owning my own coffee shop, I'll probably end up spending the rest of my life in jail for a murder I didn't commit."

"Hey," I said, feeling my heart ache for my friend. "We can't control what happens with Sea Beans, but we don't have to sit around and do nothing. I'm betting there are lots of folks who may have had a lot more motive than you."

"Like who?"

"Where there's money, there's motive. His girlfriend came into the store looking for books on contesting wills this morning," I said. "I got the impression she thought she was going to get a nice chunk of change when Charles died; she was really upset and told me that all men were 'liars.' That's worth pursuing, don't you think?"

"Huh." Her voice was changing... she sounded closer to her normal, perky self.

"And I overheard her talking with a young man at the Salty Dog at lunch. They seemed... intimate."

"Like, dating intimate?"

"Maybe," I said. "His name is John Stanton."

"How do you know that?"

"He paid for lunch with a credit card and I peeked at the receipt," I confessed.

"You're a regular Nancy Drew," she said. "How do we find out more about these people?"

"I plan to do some googling this afternoon," I said.

"Need any help at the store?" she asked.

I hesitated.

"I'll work for free," she said. "I know you're stretched, too."

"Why don't you just come hang out for a bit this after-noon?" I suggested. "I'd love to see you. And maybe we can do a little online sleuthing."

"Do you really think it will help?" she asked, sounding

unconvinced.

"You never know until you try," I said.

She sounded much better when she hung up a moment later. I called Nicholas to see if he might know any way to find out more about Amanda Duncan or John Stanton, but he wasn't answering, so I left him a voicemail asking him to call when he had a chance.

As I hung up, I heard voices behind me again.

"When is it, again?" It was the same voice I'd heard the other day. It came from the garden of the mansion behind me.

"Friday," the other voice responded. "Are you sure you're up to this? You're not going to choke again?"

Choke? Were they talking about killing someone? I turned around and quietly stepped up on the bench, trying to peer over (or through) the fence.

"Of course not," the first voice replied. "Last time was a special circumstance. I've got this time covered."

"I hope so," the other voice warned as I scrambled to peek over the fence. The voices were drifting away, and I still hadn't seen who was speaking. I jogged along the fence line until I found a plank with a knot in it. I peered through the hole, but there was a line of bushes right on the other side of the fence that made spying difficult. I caught a glimpse of a woman's dark hair and a red sweater, and a man with graying hair, but then they disappeared behind a hedge and were gone.

I watched to see if they would come out again, but there was no sign of them, and I couldn't hang out peering through the fence forever; I'd already gotten a few looks from tourists. I walked away from the fence and toward the store, wondering what to do. I could find out who lived or was staying in the house, but who would I tell? I could hardly call the police to say I thought I'd heard someone plotting a murder for this Friday. I didn't know who was plotting it, how it was supposed to take place, or who the intended victim was.

What could I do?

~

BETHANY AND CAROLINE were on opposite sides of the bookstore when I got back to the store, still thinking about the conversation I'd overheard. I was glad to see my daughter up and about, but I could tell from the icy atmosphere in the cozy, book-lined space that things at the store were far from harmonious.

"Everything okay?" I asked Bethany, who was sitting behind the register peering into her computer screen.

"Fine," she said in a tone of voice that indicated that wasn't exactly the case. "But could you take a look at this before I post it?"

I glanced at the image on the screen. It was a headshot of a brunette author in her forties, along with the cover of her most recent release, a book I didn't recognize but that looked, based on the attractive couple gracing the cover, like a historical romance. The blurb above named the time and had a little about the author's work. "Looks good," I said, glancing over at Caroline, who was shelving books rather loudly in the children's section.

"I'll put some flyers up, too," she said. "Devin and I are going to walk around town and put them up this evening. And he agreed to put the event in the library newsletter."

"That's great!" I said. "Tell him I really appreciate it. Things with you two going well?"

"We're helping each other work out some plot problems

in our books," she said, blushing a little bit.

"I'm so glad," I said. "He seems like a great guy."

As I spoke, over in the children's section, Caroline set a picture book on a shelf with a thud that made me wince for the book.

"Easy, Tiger," I said. My daughter shot me a glare that could have burnt a hole through any of the paperbacks on the shelf behind me.

"Nicholas came by a few minutes ago," Bethany said as I turned back to the register. "He wanted see if you were still on for this evening."

Ah. That could explain things. "Thanks," I said. "I'll give him a call. I'm going to head upstairs for a few minutes; if Denise comes, could you send her up?"

"Got it," Bethany said, and she gave me a shy smile. There was another loud *thunk* from the children's section. I'd have to talk with Caroline later, I decided; I wanted to do a little googling before Denise arrived.

"I'll be up in the apartment," I reiterated, and scurried up the stairs, hearing yet another *thunk* as I closed the door behind me.

I scanned my living room and kitchen and sighed. Caroline and I were going to have to have a conversation about domestic responsibilities soon, as well as about her slamming the books around in the store. Among other things I'd been putting off addressing. I had been trying to go easy on my daughter—divorce was hard—but that didn't mean it was okay for her to treat me as a maid.

I tossed the dishes in the dishwasher and tidied up the couch, then sat down at the kitchen table and pulled out my computer.

I typed in the name I'd gotten from the receipt at the Salty Dog. The top results were for people who were too old, so I switched to "images" and scanned until I found a picture that looked like the young man I'd seen at the restaurant.

I clicked on it, and was taken to an Instagram page. Unfortunately, there wasn't much there—just a profile picture of John smiling with the ocean behind him—but I was able to glean that he lived in Framingham, Massachusetts. I did another search with this new information and found a LinkedIn profile that gave me a little more to work with.

John was a computer programmer for a software company based in Boston, and he'd worked at a number of tech companies over the past few years. I scanned his list of connections and located Amanda Duncan. They had one overlap; about five years ago, they'd both worked for the same company in California.

Had they been in a relationship? I wondered. Were they still, and had Amanda been with Charles just to get his money? Had she killed him thinking she was in line to inherit, so that she and John could be together?

I searched for both of their names together, but nothing came up. As I was putting in John's name again, there was a knock on the door.

"Come in," I called, and Denise walked in. She was still wearing her Sea Beans t-shirt, her hair pulled back into a ponytail, but the ponytail was drooping. My friend looked tired, but defiant... and also worried. I stood up and closed the distance between us, pulling her into a hug.

"You okay?" I asked into her coffee-scented hair.

"No," she said, squeezing me back, then releasing me. "But I will be." She nodded toward the computer. "What did you find out?"

"Not much yet," I said. "I know Amanda used to work

with the guy who bought them lunch today, but that's about all I've dug up so far. And there's not much on Charles, either; he seems not to have existed before two years ago."

"Did you look up Chad, too?" she asked.

"The son? No, not yet."

"And what about his mom?"

"I don't know anything about her, either," I said. "Let's start with the son. Do you know his full name?"

"Chad Carsten," she said. I typed in the name. Unlike his father, Chad had quite the social media profile. We looked at LinkedIn first; he was the vice president of marketing at Venture Investments, his father's company—and the one that was trying to buy Sea Beans. His Twitter feed consisted of a series of business-inspirational quotes, and he appeared to be active on Instagram, too. I reached for my phone, opened Instagram again (I used it largely to keep an eye on the girls, but should probably set up an account for the bookstore, I reflected) and pulled up Chad's account.

"He's got about a thousand followers," Denise remarked as I scrolled through the pictures, most of which showed the young man wearing expensive-looking designer shirts, with his arm slung around a series of attractive women. In fancy restaurants, in bars, on boats... the theme was Chad with lovely female companions.

"See anyone who turns up regularly?" Denise asked.

"Not really," I said. "He seems to have played the field."

"A lot of yacht pictures," she commented as I scrolled through. His job title on Twitter was the same as on LinkedIn.

"I don't see that he works much, actually," Denise said as we scrolled through his pictures. Picture after picture of Chad on his yacht in Maine locales. "The Monkey Busi-ness," she commented, pointing to the name painted on the side of the wood-and-brass-festooned vessel. "I've seen that in the harbor lately. Must be nice to have oceanside property AND a classic yacht."

"Wonder where their money came from?" I asked.

"I was wondering the same thing," she said as we scrolled through his account. "Looks like he started his social media profiles only two years ago."

"Nothing before that?"

"Nope," she said.

I googled some more. Nothing that went beyond two years, for either Chad or Charles; neither of their LinkedIn profiles went beyond starting Venture Investments. "What, are they part of the witness relocation program?"

"I know, right? No sign of the woman who's Chad's mother, either," I said, continuing to scroll through Instagram. "Wait... here's one from Mother's Day two years ago." It showed Chad in mirrored sunglasses, posing with a glamorously made-up woman with high cheekbones and troubled-looking eyes. "Shout-out to the best mom in the world," the caption said.

"That doesn't look like Maine," Denise said, pointing to a row of palm trees in the background. The two were standing in front of a yacht that looked remarkably similar to the Monkey Business, only this one was called Happy Hour. "He certainly does like expensive yachts."

"And he looks young in that photo," I said. He was decidedly more baby-faced than in his other photos. "I'm guessing it's an old pic."

"I wonder what his mother's name is?" Denise said.

I scrolled to the next Mother's Day, but there was nothing there. "That appears to be the only mention of her," I said. "I guess he threw in with his father."

"Maybe that's because he was the one with the money,"

Denise suggested. "And the plum job."

"Although he doesn't seem to spend a lot of time at the job, does he?" I asked, looking at the pics of Chad on his yacht. There were a few of him in classic cars, too... including one in the car that had gone over the cliff. I shivered at the image of him leaning back in the driver's seat, a beautiful woman in the passenger seat beside him, one arm draped over the side of the car.

"It was a beautiful car, wasn't it?"

"It was," I said. "But Chad isn't the one who died in it. We probably need to focus more on people who might have wanted Charles out of the way. We don't know much about him, other than that he had a son and a girlfriend and liked classic cars."

"He has an ex-wife, it seems."

"But we don't know anything about her. And if she's an ex, why kill him? She probably wouldn't stand to benefit if they were divorced." I flipped back to Chad's LinkedIn page. "What do you know about the proposed takeover? It was mainly Charles involved, right?"

"Actually, no," she said. "I got the feeling it was Chad pushing things."

"Did they have any other investors with them?"

"They did once, now that you mention it, when they first came to Sea Beans to talk to Margaret," she said. "The other guy's name was Edward MacIntosh, or McIntire, or something like that. He and Chad seemed really buddy-buddy. I actually heard the father and son arguing about him once, quietly, when they thought I wasn't listening."

"When was this?"

She pursed her lips, thinking. "About two weeks ago. They were sitting outside together, and I was bussing tables."

"What was it about?"

"The father said something about this Edward MacIntosh's history drawing attention. That it was too big a risk to take, that they needed to lay low."

"Lay low?" That set my spidey senses tingling. "That's an odd phrase to use."

"I thought so, too," she said.

"Maybe they were hiding from something," I said. "That would explain why I couldn't find anything before two years ago."

I googled Edward MacIntosh; to my surprise, the first thing that popped up was a series of articles in the Boston Globe. "No wonder Daddy wasn't a fan. Look at this." I turned the laptop screen to face Denise, and her eyebrows rose.

"Edward MacIntosh suspected of embezzlement," she read. "When was this article?"

"Three years ago," I said. Apparently he'd been accused of funneling money via business loan from a small bank in Boston to a series of shell companies and then defaulting on the loans. "They dropped the charges, though, so it never went to trial."

"Wonder why?"

"I don't know," I said, scrolling through, "but he had another issue about ten years ago with a small non-profit he founded. Apparently there was misappropriation of funds."

"I wouldn't want someone like that as a partner, for sure," Denise said. "If they had so much money, though, why would they need a partner?"

"Maybe it was all for show?" I suggested. "What's the name of the chain, again?"

"Epoch Coffee," she said. I typed in the name and was directed to a swanky-looking web site. "This doesn't look very small-townish," I said, looking at the sleek logo and expensive, artfully photographed menu items. "Holy moly. Eighteen dollars for a salad? And who buys salad at a coffee house, anyway?"

"I don't know," Denise said angrily. "This whole thing is a nightmare. It's so wrong. Why not open up another location in town? Why take Sea Beans? This town can support more than one coffee shop."

I blinked, processing the implications of what she'd just said. "Denise. What you just said. I think you're right."

"What do you mean?"

"It applies to you too. Why take over Sea Beans? Why not open your own coffee house?"

"I... I couldn't do that. Compete with my old boss?"

"The boss who promised you the business, reneged and agreed to sell it to out-of-towners, and then suspended you without cause?"

"She had cause. Half of Snug Harbor thinks I pushed Charles Carsten off a cliff."

"Have you been charged with a crime?"

"No," she said.

"Did you actually push him off a cliff?"

"Of course not!"

"Then she suspended you without cause," I said. "You don't owe her allegiance."

"But... where would I put it? How would I afford it? And everyone thinks I'm a murderer. Who would buy anything from me?"

"We just have to figure out the answers to all of those questions." I looked at the screen, with its sleek logo, and wondered what the motive was for Charles and Chad Carsten to build a coffee empire.

I needed to find out a lot more about the Carstens. And

13

*W*ith Bethany and Caroline running the store, I decided to walk over to the harbor and see if I could take a closer look at Monkey Business, the yacht in all of Chad's photos. I was hoping to have a chance to run into the man himself and ask him some questions. It was hard figuring out what had happened when I had no personal connection to any of the people involved. Was there some way to manufacture one?

It was a short walk down to the town pier. The tide was high, so there was no sea glass to distract me, and my mind kept moving to the rumrunner's secret stash. As I walked, I spied the island Nicholas and I had visited the other day. With everything that was going on with Denise, I'd forgotten to pursue that any further. Maybe we could make plans for the next step during our date?

I was still thinking about Nicholas as I got to the pier. Sure enough, Monkey Business was moored in the first berth, its brass railing and wood decking gleaming in the late afternoon sun. As I watched, a young woman in a blue knit shirt and khakis stepped out onto the deck with a rag and a spray bottle. As I leaned against the dock railing, she went to work cleaning the windows.

"Nice boat," I called out after a moment.

The young woman turned and shielded her eyes from the sun with a hand, smiling at me. "It is, isn't it? I love these old vessels. I'm so glad this one is being taken care of." She patted the cabin wall affectionately.

"Is it yours?"

She snorted. "I wish. I'm just crew, unfortunately. Hopefully someday I'll be able to captain one of these, but for now, I'm just a deckhand."

"Have you been doing it long?"

"About six months," she said. "Although I'm not sure how long I'll be able to keep this job."

"What do you mean?"

She walked toward me, glancing over her shoulder as she leaned over the rail. "You heard about the guy who went over the cliff a couple days ago?"

"Everyone in town's heard about that," I said. "Why?"

"That was my boss," she said in a low voice.

"Wow," I said. "What do you think happened?"

She glanced over her shoulder again. "Well, I don't think it was an accident."

"Because the brake lines were cut?" I said without thinking, then added, "That's what I heard happened, anyway."

"That's what happened," she confirmed. "I heard Chad —my boss' son—say it yesterday."

"Any idea who did it?"

"Well, Charles's ex-wife marched up the dock last week and boarded without asking, demanding to see him."

"Wait... what? How do you know that's who she was?"

"She asked if he'd forgotten they'd been married and had a kid together. He didn't deny it, so I assumed..."

"That makes sense. So Charles was here?"

"He was," she confirmed. "When he stepped out of the main cabin, he looked like he was seeing a ghost. He asked how she found him, and she told him his expensive hobbies had caught up with him. He hustled her inside, but before that, she told him if he didn't take care of her properly, she was going to blow the lid on everything."

"What does that mean?"

"I don't know, but he seemed... scared, almost. I've never seen him look like that before. He was usually quiet and kind of in-command, but he looked like a kid caught with his hand in the cookie jar, if you know what I mean."

"I do," I said. "What about Chad?"

"Junior? He's the playboy, likes to show off. Kind of new money-ish, if you know what I mean. Charles... he liked nice things, but he tended to stay under the radar. Not a lot of visitors, except for his girlfriend."

"Was she here when the ex-wife showed up?"

"No, thankfully for her. She didn't like the Monkey Business too much, probably because Chad was always trolling for women in town and bringing them back to show off. He was in that hot tub on the top deck every night."

"I heard they were looking to buy some coffee shop in town."

"They've been running a whole bunch of coffee shops. From what I could hear, it was Chad's idea, and his dad was funding it."

"I wonder how well they're doing at it. I mean, can coffee houses fund a seaside house and a yacht?"

"I don't know," she said, "but they seemed to have plenty. Charles did, anyway. Chad acted like a player, but the money was his daddy's."

"So you've worked for them for six months?"

"Yes, almost," she said.

"Is it a good gig?"

"It's good experience," she said. "I'm hoping to be first mate soon. Or at least I was," she said, shoulders drooping a little bit.

"Why wouldn't you be?"

"Well, with Mr. Carsten gone... Like I said, I'm not sure how long I'll get to keep this job."

"You're not sure they'll keep the boat?"

"I don't know if Chad will inherit it, or sell it, or what."

"Does Chad have any siblings?"

"Not that I know of," she said. "They were arguing about the will a few weeks ago, over drinks."

"Who was?"

"Charles and his girlfriend. She said if he wasn't going to marry her, he should at least do something to provide for her."

Interesting. "How did it shake out?"

"I don't know, but she looked pretty satisfied at breakfast."

Had he agreed to change his will and then not gotten around to it? Did she think she'd been written in and then offed him? Was his ex-wife jealous when she found out about his new girlfriend? Or did his son find out he stood to lose at least part of his fortune and kill his father before he had a chance to change the will?

"Did his son know about the argument with the girlfriend?" I asked.

"He wasn't here, so I don't think so," she said. "Amanda wouldn't have told him, I don't think. But the two of them don't like each other." She twisted the rag in her hand. "I don't know why I'm telling you all of this. I guess it's good to talk to someone about it."

"I get that," I said. "Out of curiosity, do you know if Charles' ex-wife was staying in town?"

"I saw her a couple days ago when I was buying provisions at the grocery store," she said. "She didn't recognize me."

So the ex-wife was in town. And had likely been in town when Charles died. Had he been scared of her because of something she might say? I wondered. Or something he was afraid she might do?

Like murder him?

"Do you know what she's called?" I asked.

"Josie Cole," the deckhand said. "He called her Josie. She said 'That's Mrs. Cole to you.'"

Josie Cole, I thought, making a mental note of it. As she spoke, there were voices from behind me, and she suddenly started. "I've got to go," she said abruptly, turning and hurrying back to the window she had been working on

I tuned to see Chad Carsten walking toward the Monkey Business, a pretty young woman with a variety of nose rings and a midriff-baring top leaning into him. She was talking happily, but he was focused on me, eyes narrowed.

"Can I help you with something?" he asked, interrupting his girlfriend. She stiffened and stopped talking.

"Oh, no," I said. "I was just admiring your yacht. I love that you're taking such good care of her; she's just beautiful, and obviously in mint condition."

"Thanks," he said, relaxing a little bit. Then a little wrinkle appeared between his eyebrows. "Don't I know you from somewhere?"

"I don't think so," I said, deciding not to mention our meeting at the bookstore. "I'm Max. I live in town."

"Chad Carsten," he said. The woman on his arm looked at him expectantly, as if waiting to be introduced, but he ignored her. "I'm afraid I have things to attend to," he said, then walked past me and boarded the yacht. The deckhand, who had been so relaxed and chatty a few minutes earlier, turned, stood up straight, and said "Good afternoon, sir," in a quiet voice. He nodded and walked past her, his girlfriend still hanging on his arm, and disappeared into the cabin.

Once the door had closed, I said, "Hey. Thanks for chatting... I hope I didn't get you into trouble."

"Please don't share anything I said," she replied in a low, anxious voice. "I think I work for him now, and I can't afford to lose this job until I've found something else."

"Got it," I said. "Good luck with everything."

She nodded, her shoulders now hunched and a worried frown on her young face, and sprayed another window as I turned and walked to the boardwalk, thinking of everything I had just learned.

Josie Cole.

If she was staying in town, I planned to find her.

I HEADED HOME NEXT, checking in with Bethany and Caroline and then hurrying upstairs, giving Winston, who was curled up on the couch, a quick belly rub and a potty break outside before opening up my computer. Winston was disappointed in the short outing and stood at the door, whining.

"We'll go farther later, Buddy," I said. I'd deal with him... and with Caroline, who still hadn't tidied up... later.

First I did a search for Josie Cole, but couldn't find anyone online with that name who resembled the woman I'd seen in Chad Carsten's Instagram picture.

Then I switched to the Chamber of Commerce website

for Snug Harbor and printed a list of hotels in the area, hoping she hadn't decided to rent a cottage. I picked up the phone and called the first one, the Anchorage Motel, and asked to speak with Josie Cole.

"I'm sorry, there's no one here by that name," responded the desk clerk, so I thanked her and dialed the next on the list.

I had gone through ten of them and was beginning to feel like I was barking up the wrong tree when a young man at the Snug Harbor Inn said, "I'm sorry, but you just missed her; I saw her leaving a few minutes ago. Can I take a message?"

"No, thank you," I said. "I'll catch up with her later." I hung up, gave Winston a treat, and looked up the Snug Harbor Inn. They had a restaurant, I was pleased to see. I called Nicholas.

"How would you like it if we had our dinner at the Snug Harbor Inn tonight?" I asked.

"Is there some kind of special occasion?"

"Well, time with you is always a special occasion," I said, "but I thought we might plan our next outing over dinner... and maybe run into Charles Carsten's ex-wife."

"You mean the ex-wife of the guy who died? Why would we run into her there?"

"She's staying at the inn," I told him, recounting what I had learned from the deckhand of the Monkey Business that afternoon. "Her name is Josie Cole, and apparently she and Charles had a bit of a kerfuffle on the Monkey Business last week."

"What's the Monkey Business?"

"The Carstens' yacht," I said.

"How did you find that out?"

"I'm gregarious," I said.

"I love your gregariousness. You always keep things interesting."

I laughed. "You're pretty wonderful, you know that?"

He chuckled. "I'm not sure opposing counsel on the case I'm trying next week agrees with you, but thanks for the props."

I laughed and hung up, feeling a little bit optimistic about things for the first time since Denise told me she was a suspect.

      *T*he Snug Harbor Inn was a gorgeous mansion nestled into a cove on the south side of Snug Harbor, a little bit away from the bustle of town. The house was white painted clapboard with a grand porch that extended all along the front, with baskets of red impatiens and dark green ivy and cozy-looking rocking chairs with plump cushions for guests to enjoy the view of the stunning Maine coast.

"Maybe we should get a room here some weekend," Nicholas suggested as we pulled up in the gravel parking lot a little bit down the hill.

"That would be amazing," I said.

"Maybe for your birthday. Unless you want to go further afield?"

"How could anyplace be more beautiful than this?" I asked as I got out of the car and smoothed down my dress.

I stopped for a moment to admire yet again the deep blue water, the pearly white of the breaking surf, and the brilliant, sunset-hued sky. A breeze kicked up as I stood there, bringing the faint scent of roses on the cool, salt-laden air, along with just a hint of balsam fir. It was clean and fresh and invigorating, and once again I thanked my lucky stars that I got to live here... and as Nicholas rounded the car and put his arm around me, giving me a squeeze, I added thanks again that I had met this handsome, kind, absolutely entrancing man. He gave me a gentle kiss on the lips and took in my made-up face and styled hair. "Have I told you recently how beautiful you are?"

I blushed; after twenty-plus years of a less-than-ideal marriage, I wasn't used to compliments. "Thanks," I replied, feeling a little like a teenager.

He gave me another tender kiss, then took my hand. "Shall we?"

"I'd love to," I said, and together we walked up the steps and across the front porch to the door of the Snug Harbor Inn.

The lobby somehow managed to be both grand and cozy at the same time. A massive oak staircase was the center-piece of the room, with ornate carving and a deep blue velvet carpet runner over the gleaming wood steps. Two cozy nooks with overstuffed chairs overlooked views of the front porch and the green, manicured lawn outside, and the front desk was just that: an old-fashioned desk that would have looked at home in a banker's office, except for the addi-tion of an exquisite bouquet of roses and larkspur in a crystal vase. Mounted on the wall behind the desk was a walnut board of about twenty old-fashioned keys on hooks. I wondered which one belonged to Josie Cole.

"We're here for dinner," I said.

"The restaurant is through there," the young woman said in a pleasant voice, pointing to a pair of open double doors just to the left of the grand staircase. "Do you have a reservation?"

"Do we need one?" Nicholas asked.

"It's usually advisable, but I think we've got some tables open tonight. The host should be able to seat you; he's right through those doors."

"Thanks," Nicholas said, and with his hand on the small of my back, we walked from the hotel lobby into the restaurant.

The smell of fresh bread permeated the air, and several couples were seated at tables around the restaurant. White tablecloths, candles, and small vases of flowers decorated the tables, and the pleasant-faced young host led us to a table by a window, with a view of the now sunset-gilded water caressing the granite rocks of the cove behind the restaurant. He handed us heavy, leather-bound menus as I scanned the restaurant, looking for any sign of Josie.

"Is she here?" Nicholas asked me.

"If she is, I don't recognize her," I said. "I only know her from a photo. We may have to come up with some other plan."

"Like getting a room?" he asked with a saucy wink. He reached across the table and enveloped my hand in his, and I felt my pulse pick up.

"I was thinking staking out the lobby, but that sounds a lot more fun," I replied, surprised at the feelings welling up in me in the presence of my new beau. For a moment, I let the rest of my troubles melt away and focused on the handsome man across the table from me... the one who made me feel like I was the center of his universe.

He took my hand and guided it to his lips, planting a soft kiss, and then set it back down on the tablecloth, still folded in his. "Okay. What are you thinking for wine? I'm in the mood for seafood... maybe a nice Sancerre?"

I felt myself tighten; I didn't have the money for nice

wine right now, much less fancy seafood dinners. But we were here on my account. "Maybe just a glass," I suggested.

"This is my treat," he reiterated.

"Are you sure?" I asked, opening the menu and glancing down at the prices, which were a bit out of my current budget, to say the least.

"Like I said earlier, you're building a business. When your empire is up and running, you can treat me."

"Thank you," I said, feeling myself relax again. "I love Sancerre."

"Excellent," he said, squeezing my hand before releasing it and opening the menu. "That's settled. Now... I'm thinking maybe scallops. And I know how much you love lobster... I'm thinking we should start with Clams Casino, though."

"Sounds good to me," I said, my mouth already watering at the thought of baked clams on the half-shell, dotted with butter and bacon bits and all manner of good things. It was turning out to be a rather clam-heavy day for me... not to mention calories. Tomorrow would have to involve a lot more salad.

"So," he said, once we'd placed our order. "Let's talk about the next steps with our treasure hunt."

"I feel like all we're doing is finding places they used to use to store things," I said. "I'm beginning to think there really isn't any hidden treasure."

"Satterthwaite had to do something with his earnings," Nicholas pointed out. "From everything I've researched, your store was the only piece of property he owned, and he didn't seem to have amassed a public fortune in any other way."

"Maybe he lost it all in the crash?" I suggested.

"Maybe," he said. "But I still think we should exhaust all our options. Think of what you could do with a windfall."

"I could help Denise start her own business," I said.

"I was thinking more of your business, but that would be great, too. Is she thinking of starting a coffee house of her own?"

"I suggested it today," I said. "I think there's room in Snug Harbor for more than one coffee place."

"It's a good idea," he said. "What about the building next to yours?"

I blinked. "Why didn't I think of that? It's right next to the bookstore, and everyone keeps telling me I need a coffee house. We could market them together, somehow. Although it is a bit off the beaten path..." I mused.

"Put a big deck with a view of the ocean off the back and I'll bet you get lots of takers. And if she can work it out with one of the tour boat companies to sell tickets at her shop, and then get a discount on coffee..."

"And that would draw a lot more people down to Seaside Cottage Books, too," I said, feeling excitement well in me. "That's brilliant."

"It's just an idea," he said. "I have no idea what she'd have to do to make that building workable... or how much it would cost to rent or buy the space."

"It's definitely worth checking out," I said. "She's always wanted to put her own spin on the coffee house thing; I know she has lots of ideas, but Margaret hasn't always been open to them."

"And I'd rather go to a local coffee shop than a chain," he said.

"I don't know if everyone would agree with you," I said, "but that appeals to me, too. I'll talk with Denise about it." Then the memory of why she was no longer in line to take over Sea Beans returned, settling over me like a lead blanket. "We still need to figure out what happened to Charles

Carsten, though, or she's not going to be able to do anything other than make license plates."

"Do they still do that in jail?"

"I don't know, but I don't want her to have to find out." As I spoke, the waiter returned with a chilled bottle of white wine. When Nicholas tasted it and gave him the okay, he filled our glasses and left the bottle in an ice bucket at the end of the table.

"To getting Denise off the hook and into a coffee house of her own," I said, lifting my glass and admiring the pale yellow wine.

"And to finding Josiah Satterthwaite's treasure," Nicholas added. Just as we were about to touch glasses, I heard my name.

"Max! Is that you?"

I turned to see Kirsten standing at the host stand, my ex-husband behind her.

15

"*O*h, boy," I murmured under my breath, and then half-heartedly waved back at her. She took that as an invitation and headed our way, Ted—I mean, Theodore —in her wake.

"I'm so glad to run into you. I've been dying to try this place, but I forgot to make a reservation and all the tables are full." I glanced around; while Nicholas and I had been talking, the restaurant had filled up. "Do you mind if we join you? I wouldn't ask, but there's nowhere to sit, and Theodore had his heart set on a bowl of their lobster bisque..."

"Well..." I said.

"Max won't mind, I'm sure," my ex said, pulling up a chair next to me as Kirsten settled herself in beside Nicholas.

Once she'd situated herself, she turned to Nicholas. "Where are my manners! We haven't even introduced ourselves. I'm Kirsten Anderson," she said, "and this is my boyfriend, Theodore. He and Max used to be married, although I'm sure you know that."

"Nice to see you," Nicholas said politely.

"How do you know Max, again?" Ted asked, narrowing his eyes a hair.

"We knew each other growing up, actually," Nicholas said.

"That's wonderful." Kirsten, who was looking glamorous as usual in a leather pencil skirt paired with a silky blouse, leaned forward, her French-manicured fingers toying with the gorgeous gold pendant she wore. It brought out the glow in her tanned skin, and I found myself experiencing a small rush of jealousy. Had Ted bought it for her? I wondered, stealing a glance at him. Even though I'd picked out one of my best dresses, I found myself feeling frumpy next to Kirsten, and nervously checked to see if my earrings —small pearls—were still in place. "Did you stay in touch over the years, or did you recently reconnect?" she asked.

"We recently reconnected," Nicholas said, putting his arm around me and pulling me in toward him. The gesture relieved some of my anxiety, and I turned to give him a grateful smile. "I can't believe I let her get away the first time; I won't make that mistake again."

"That's so romantic," Kirsten gushed, but I couldn't help noticing her long-lashed eyes flickering briefly to Ted, whose eyebrows were almost all the way up to his receding hairline. Which did look like it was a little sparser than it had been when we were together, I noted. "Don't you think, sweetheart?" she asked, putting a possessive hand of her own on his knee. But Ted was focused on Nicholas.

"So, you're dating?" he asked with his customary tact.

"We are," Nicholas said, giving me another squeeze. "I'm glad she decided to take the risk and move back to Snug Harbor. And keeping the bookstore going is a bonus."

Ted sniffed. "With technology moving on, I don't see

how a bricks-and-mortar bookstore is ever going to be a long-term game plan for success, but it's good she's pursuing her dreams," he said, as if I weren't even at the table. "She always was more of a dreamer than a businesswoman, though."

"Really? That hasn't been my experience at all," Nicholas said. "I think she's doing an amazing job at the bookstore."

My ex-husband gave him a tight grimace. Beside him, Kirsten was still smiling, but her face looked brittle, and there was a hardness around her mascaraed eyes that told me Ted was about knee-deep in hot water and wading deeper. "How about you, Nick? What do you do for a living?"

Nicholas smiled politely and said, "I'm an attorney, actually."

"So you sue people for a living," Ted said.

Before Nicholas could respond, our waitress appeared at Ted's elbow. "Welcome," she said. "Can I get you two something to drink? Do you need the wine list? Or should I bring two more glasses?"

"Well, since you already have the bottle... why don't you bring some more glasses?" Ted said, without consulting Nicholas or me.

"If that's okay with you two, of course," Kirsten said, putting a hand on Ted's arm.

"Of course," Nicholas said politely, but I could hear the chill in his voice. I wanted to tell him I was sorry, or get up and just go to another table, but the restaurant was full. Kirsten telegraphed something like an apology to me with her eyes, and I grimaced in response. As I was fishing for a topic of conversation that did not involve my budding relationship with Nicholas, Kirsten came to my rescue.

"Have you found out anything else about that man who died?" she asked.

"Actually, I have," I said as the waitress returned with two extra glasses and filled them both, almost draining the bottle. "And that's why we're here."

"What?" She leaned forward, eyes alight. "Tell me."

I leaned toward her, talking in a low voice, as Ted took a hearty swig of wine. "Apparently he does have an ex-wife, and she's in town... or at least she was last week. Her name is Josie Cole, according to a deckhand on his yacht, and when I called around town, they said she was staying here."

"So you're here to try to spot her," Kirsten said. "Do you know what she looks like?"

"I found a picture of her on her son's Instagram," I said. "At least I think it's her; he posted it on Mother's Day and said she was the best mom ever."

"It had better be his mom, or he'll have some explaining to do," Kirsten said as I pulled out my phone and pulled up Chad Carsten's Instagram feed, scrolling through until I found the photo.

"This is her," I said, showing her the picture.

"What are you going to do if you see her?" Kirsten asked.

"I'm not sure yet," I said. "I'd like to talk to her, but I don't really know how to broach it. 'Hi, I heard you were married to the guy who fell off a cliff the other day' just doesn't seem like the ideal ice-breaker."

She laughed, a throaty, guttural laugh that made her more likable, somehow. "No, best not to lead with that. Maybe get to talking about your recent divorce?" she suggested.

"To get her talking about her own divorce," I said. "That's a great idea."

"Just because she's staying at the hotel doesn't mean

she's going to eat at the restaurant," Ted pointed out unhelpfully.

I resisted the urge to roll my eyes. Instead, I gave him a tight smile and sipped my wine, trying to release the tension that had built in me since Ted and Kirsten had sat down across from us. It bothered me how little it took to get a rise out of me. I looked forward to a time when he was no longer able to get under my skin with such ease. It was a little embarrassing, actually, having Nicholas as an audience to those old, automatic responses. I wanted to move into a new life, not stay mired in old patterns.

"Is that her?" Nicholas asked, nodding toward the bar.

Ted swiveled, and Kirsten turned more casually. Sure enough, an attractive woman with an aquiline nose and dark hair pulled up in a French twist had sat down at the bar and was examining a menu.

"Looks like her," Kirsten said, her eyes calculating.

"How do we approach her?" I asked.

"Leave it to me," Kirsten said, half-draining her glass of Sancerre.

"What do you mean?" I asked, but by the time I finished answering the question, she had stood up and was striding toward the entrance.

16

"Where is she going?" Nicholas asked.

"She's going to get the goods," Ted said, finishing the contents of his own glass and reaching for the bottle. Once he'd poured the rest into his glass, he glanced back toward the entrance, where Kirsten was strolling in as if she'd just arrived. As we watched, she slid onto a bar stool two down from Josie and flagged the bartender.

Now what? Nicholas and I were here for a romantic date... but also to see if we could find Josie Cole. Now that we had found Josie, Kirsten had left my ex with us to go and interrogate her, without talking to me about it.

I didn't want to abandon Nicholas, but I didn't want to miss the opportunity to make contact with Josie.

"What do I do?" I asked Nicholas in a low voice.

"Follow your gut," he replied with an encouraging smile.

"I feel bad leaving you alone..."

"Follow your gut," he repeated, and gave my hand a squeeze under the table.

I smiled and nodded slightly, then announced, "I'll be back."

"You don't need to go," Ted objected. "Kirsten has it handled. She's amazing at getting info out of people."

I ignored him, standing up and walking to the entrance just as Kirsten began engaging Josie in conversation at the bar. I walked out to the lobby, took a few deep breaths as I gazed out at the stretch of water leading out to the gulf, then turned and headed back into the restaurant as if I were arriving for the first time.

Kirsten was laughing, presumably at something Josie had said, when I approached her at the bar.

"Kirsten!" I said, widening my eyes. "I had no idea you were in Snug Harbor!"

Kirsten turned and blinked, her smile faltering for a moment. "Max? What are you doing here?"

"Just a whim," I said, reaching for the bar stool between Kirsten and Josie. "Mind if I join you?" I asked, sitting down before she could respond. "Who's your friend?"

"I'm Josie Cole," said the woman with the aquiline nose, a little bit coolly.

"Max Sayers," I said. "Are you new to town? Or just visiting?"

"Visiting," she said. "I had a bit of business to take care of."

"What kind of business?" I asked, flagging down the bartender. "I could kill for a glass of wine... do you need a refill?"

"Sure," Josie said with a slight smile. "Vodka soda," she told the bartender.

"And a glass of dry white for me, please," I added. "You need anything, Kirsten?"

"I'm good, thanks," she said, taking a sip of the pink drink the bartender had just set in front of her: a Cape Cod, of course. Ted's new favorite drink.

"So," I said, turning to face Josie. "What do you think of Snug Harbor?"

"Well," she said, "it's beautiful, but it's not really my cup of tea."

"I gather you're not here just for the lobster," I said.

"No," she replied. "Just a bit of an issue with my ex."

"Divorce?" I gave her a sympathetic smile. "I totally get it. Mine was final last year, and I'm still recovering."

"Oh, he didn't bother divorcing me," she said. "He just took off, cleaned out the accounts, and started a new life with a different name."

"Ouch," I said. "That sounds horrible."

"Oh, it was," she said. "The house got foreclosed on because I couldn't pay. And even my son went with him."

"He took your kid?"

"Well, technically he's a young adult," she said, taking a big sip of her drink, "but he went with him. Completely vanished."

"But why?" I asked. "Did he not want to split the estate with you?"

"He was in legal trouble," she said, her voice laced with bitterness and disappointment. "So he just took everything and left me holding the bag."

"I am so sorry," I said. "Have you talked with him since he left?"

"I lost track of him for two years," she said. "But I finally figured out how to track him down. I confronted him last week."

"How did you do it?" Kirsten interjected from behind me. "Did you hire a private investigator?"

"No," she said. "I couldn't afford it. I tracked him down through his cars."

"His cars?" I asked.

Josie took another long sip of her drink. "He has a thing for antique cars; it's like an obsession. I think he cared about his cars more than he cared about me; I once got sunscreen on the leather in one of them, and he about blew a gasket." She shook her head, her face tight with anger. "I knew he wouldn't be able to give them up, or stop showing them off. Sure enough, I found his favorite car listed on a web site for enthusiasts. And it led me to Snug Harbor."

"So your ex lives here," Kirsten said.

"Lived here," she corrected. "He died a few days ago. Ironically, in the car he loved so much." She let out a bitter laugh. "At least they went together."

"I'm so sorry," I said. "I know it must have been hard, but still... you spent years together. Are you okay?"

"I'm... I'm numb, actually," she said. "I don't know what to think."

"What about your son?" Kirsten asked. "Have you located him?"

"Oh, I have," she said, mouth twisting. "I wish it were different, but he's cut from the same cloth as his father. Getting into the same kind of trouble..." She trailed off.

"Trouble?" I asked.

"Never mind," she said, and I could sense that her guard was up. "I shouldn't be talking about all of this. It's just... it's been a lot."

"I'm so sorry," I said.

"What about you? You said you recently divorced. How has that been?"

"It's been an adjustment," I said. "We have twin daughters together, and I think it's been particularly hard for one of them, especially now that her dad and I are dating other people."

"Does your ex have a girlfriend?" she asked. "Mine had

tons, even while we were together. I found that out after he left."

"He does," I said, very aware of Kirsten beside me; her posture was very erect as she took a tiny sip of her Cape Cod. "She's very nice," I said, being kind. "I hope she and my ex find happiness together."

"It's funny, isn't it?" Josie mused. "We were so good together when we started, but over time... everything just changed. And you hit a point where there's so much damage done—little cuts, just day-to-day things that never get repaired—that there's just no going back."

I thought about the slow, painful death of my own marriage. The hundreds and thousands of tiny grievances that didn't seem like a big enough deal to bring up at the time they happened. And how they grew over time, until they morphed into something so huge and intractable we couldn't see past it to find each other anymore. "I know exactly what you mean," I said, and glanced past Josie toward my ex-husband... and my new love interest. Could I avoid the same fate by going into a new relationship carrying the wisdom of the one that failed, with more atten-tion to clearing the small hurts before they became big ones? I shook myself a little bit and turned my attention back to Josie. Her eyebrows were delicate and winged at the top corner, but her eyes tilted down, and there was no sparkle in them. There had been, in the photo I'd seen of her with her son, but those were happier times. "Did you date after your husband left?" I asked.

She looked down at the floor, and I her cheeks flushed just a little bit, as if the question had embarrassed her. "I was too hurt and angry," she said. "Ashamed, I guess. I didn't think anyone would want me, if I'm honest." Her voice shook a little, and had a raw edge... there was anger, there, too. Enough anger to kill her ex-husband? I wondered.

I looked at her. If she didn't feel as if anyone would want her, then God help the rest of us. She was beautiful, trim, eloquent, well put together... "I imagine they would be lining up around the block," I said, meaning it.

"Maybe," she said, unconvinced.

"You just have to move on," Kirsten said from behind me. "Just because you were married to a terrible person doesn't mean the rest of your life is over. I mean, I've found love again, and I think we're grateful our old relationships ended."

I turned to look at my ex-husband's girlfriend, and my eyebrows rose seemingly of their own accord.

"Was your boyfriend's ex that awful?" I asked before I could help myself.

It was Kirsten's time to blush. "Well... not awful, but he wasn't happy. He wasn't getting his needs met."

"I imagine she wasn't either," I mused. "I mean, I know in my marriage, it was a little bit hard to feel cared for when my husband worked eighty hours a week and forgot my birthday every other year."

"Yes, well, every relationship is different," Kirsten said. "I imagine he must have had some needs that y... that his ex-wife wasn't able to fill. I mean, he loves to travel, but he and his ex never went anywhere."

"Maybe that was because he always said he was on deadline and didn't have the time," I bit back.

"I'm sorry," Josie said; I'd almost forgotten she was there. "Am I interrupting something?"

"No, of course not," I said, remembering myself. "I guess all this talk of divorce makes me feel defensive. Anyway... what now? Now that he's gone, are you going to have some kind of... settlement, at least? Regain some of the property he stole?"

"We'll see," she said. "There may be some legal issues, but I'm hoping there'll be enough to at least help me pay a small mortgage."

"And your son?" I asked.

"I haven't seen him in two years," she said flatly. "He knew where to find me. He just didn't."

"Do you know where he is now?" Kirsten asked.

She nodded.

"Are you going to talk to him?"

"I don't know," she said. "I guess I should let him know I'm here, at least."

"He doesn't know?" Kirsten asked.

"Not unless his father told him," Josie said. She sighed. "I'll think on it. I do love him. I'm just still really hurt."

"I get that," I said.

She picked up her phone. "I don't even know his number," she said. "But I know where he lives."

"Talk to him," I said, speaking from the heart. "You won't know until you do."

She took another sip of her vodka tonic. "You know, I think you're right. If it's bothering me, I should take steps to make amends." She put down her drink and stood up. "Thank you, ladies. I feel like this meeting was meant to be."

She put a ten-dollar bill on the bar, gave us a parting smile, and strode out of the bar.

"Well," Kirsten said. "I had that handled, but I feel like that was productive. I would have gotten more out of her on my own, though."

"Maybe," I said, shrugging. "But I needed to talk to her."

"Do you think she killed him?"

I thought of her bitterness, and of that flare of anger I'd seen. "I don't think so. But I can't say for sure. Leaving her with their son and all their money? I can't say I wouldn't have killed him if I were in her situation," I half-joked.

Kirsten's manicured eyebrow twitched.

"Kidding," I said. "But I do hope things go well with her son."

"Unless she was the murderer, and decides to kill him too, for deserting her."

I blinked. "I hadn't thought of that."

"That's because you're not a mystery author," she said, flagging down the waiter and asking for the check to be sent to our table. "Shall we?" she asked, in a rather frostier tone than usual.

"Of course," I said, sliding off the barstool and back to our table for the rest of our no-longer-very-romantic dinner.

17

"Well, that was... interesting," Nicholas said once we'd paid the check (at least Kirsten offered to split it) and said our goodbyes. "What exactly happened up at the bar?"

Kirsten had given the table the overview of what we learned, but hadn't mentioned the bit of verbal sparring. "It got a little heated there for a minute," I admitted.

"I could tell," he said, pulling me into him. "Did she hit a nerve?"

"She did," I said. "Talking about how her boyfriend's ex-wife just wasn't meeting his needs. I got a little defensive... I almost outed us, to be honest." I sighed. "I guess I'm still angry."

"You and Ted were together for two decades," he said gently, kissing me on top of the head as we walked along the inn porch. "I think that's perfectly normal. Want to sit for a minute?" he asked, gesturing to a pair of rocking chairs overlooking the now-moonlit water.

"Sure," I said, and he reached for my hand as we sat

down together, squeezing it. "I still can't believe they just waltzed over and sat down with us."

"I think that was mainly Kirsten," he said. "Your ex looked like he'd rather be just about anywhere else on the planet."

"He didn't hesitate to reach for the wine, though."

"Wouldn't you?" Nicholas said, and I couldn't help but laugh. "He's a nice man, though. Totally not a fit for you, but pleasant enough."

"It's a little frustrating that now all of a sudden he's up for all these adventures he never wanted to do while we were married. I mean, it's not that I want to do them with him, but where was all that when we were together?"

"Maybe he's trying to improve the next time around," Nicholas suggested.

I sighed. "You're probably right. I know I am."

"I think you're amazing," he said. "And I think somewhere inside, he must be kicking himself for letting you go."

I looked over at Nicholas, feeling a wave of absolute gratitude for this moment with this man. "I'm so glad he did, though," I said, and leaned in to kiss him.

As we kissed, a car swerved into the gravel drive and crunched to a stop, askew in one of the parking spaces. The car door swung open and a woman emerged, looking unsteady on her feet. She slammed it and hurtled toward the inn's steps, a hand to her face as she stumbled up the short stairway. Her formerly impeccable French twist now slewed to the side, and she let out a little sob before opening the door and disappearing inside.

"Was that Josie Cole?" Nicholas asked.

"It was," I confirmed.

"If she had a reunion with her son, I'm guessing it didn't go very well," he said.

I grimaced. "I'm afraid you may be right." I sighed. "I wish I could go ask her what happened."

"Maybe we can come back for happy hour tomorrow," he suggested. "After all, we never did make a plan for our next treasure-hunting mission, did we? Although I thought I might map out all the coordinates we found and see if anything looks more likely than others," he suggested.

"Maybe we should do another search of the basement," I said. "See if we missed anything."

"I can't see how," he said, "but if it's time with you, I'm game!"

I laughed and gave him a kiss. "Where have you been all my life?"

"Waiting for you," he said, kissing me back, and for a little bit, at least, all my problems seemed to fade away.

AN HOUR OR SO LATER, I looked down from the balcony outside my apartment door and waved as Nicholas pulled out of the driveway behind the bookstore. He blew me a kiss before driving away, and I walked in to find my daughter sitting on the couch watching TV, Winston snuggled in next to her. He wagged at me, but decided to stay put.

"What's for dinner?" she asked.

"You didn't eat yet? There's plenty in the fridge. How did things go at the store this evening?"

"Mostly quiet," she said. "Where were you, anyway?"

"Just out for dinner."

She grunted, then begrudgingly said, "How was it?"

"It was... interesting," I said.

"What does that mean?" she asked, narrowing her eyes at me.

"It was just a nice evening," I said, deciding not to mention the whole dad-and-his-girlfriend thing. Or the questioning of Charles Carsten's ex-wife. Or was it widow? "I think I'm heading to bed. I'm on the schedule to open the store tomorrow; what are you up to?"

She shrugged. "I don't know."

"Don't we have that author reading this Friday?" I asked. "We should put out some flyers tomorrow; can you walk through town and post some?"

"Wouldn't just posting it on social media be easier?"

"We don't have that many followers yet," I pointed out. "Although maybe we could invite some local businesses to follow us?"

"But don't we want to target tourists and locals?"

"If they follow us, they can see and repost our events, right?" I asked.

"I guess," she said, obviously more interested in the drama on the screen than anything else.

I tried to hide my frustration—after all, she was dealing with a lot, with the divorce, her dad dating and sharing her family home with another woman, her uncertainty about her future... it *was* a lot. Instead of erupting at her, I walked over, gave her a kiss on the head, and asked her to be sure Winston went out again before she went to bed.

Sometimes you have to pick your battles.

THE RUMBLE of thunder woke me the next morning, and I opened my eyes to raindrops lashing the panes of my bedroom window. The sunny, bright world of yesterday had been replaced by a moody, gray morning. I stood up and wrapped my bathrobe around me, peering out at Snug Island, which was wreathed in swirling gray mist this morning, the stretch of water between the mainland and the island gunmetal gray and pocked with raindrops.

I padded out of the bedroom and into the kitchen. Caroline was asleep on the couch, Winston still curled up next to her, and a plate with the crumbs of what looked like it might have been a tuna sandwich lay on the table next to a half-empty bottle of Coke.

Thunder grumbled again as I filled the coffee maker with fresh ground coffee and water, then turned it on. By the time the aroma of fresh-brewed coffee wafted into the apartment, I had finished getting dressed for the day and checked my phone for messages.

"Loved being with you last night," Nicholas had texted while I was making coffee. "Let's do it again soon!"

I felt my heart squeeze, and butterflies fluttered in my stomach. It was a little like being seventeen again, I thought as I reread the message and tucked the phone into my jeans pocket. I spent a few extra minutes in front of the mirror, just in case Nicholas decided to stop by that day, putting on a touch of blush and mascara and adding a bit of tinted lip balm, then chose some simple silver earrings to complement the gray cowl-neck sweater I had slipped on. I added a pendant necklace and a spritz of perfume and looked at myself in the mirror.

My hazel eyes looked back at me from under dark brows. Two faint creases grooved the center of my forehead, and my jawline had softened over the years, but my hair was still full and only slightly shot with gray. I wasn't twenty-five anymore, but I liked the way I looked, I decided... even if I had put on a little bit of what a friend called "the suburban donut" around the middle as the years had passed. It had been decades since I'd taken the time to care for my appearance, and even though I hadn't spent hours doing my hair and my face, taking a few minutes to add a touch of blush and mascara brightened my face and made me feel... like I valued myself. It wasn't for Nicholas that I had put on earrings, I realized as I swept a stray hair behind my ear and turned from the mirror.

It was for me.

THE MORNING WAS slow at the store, and I spent a lot of it trying to find out more about Josie Cole. Unfortunately, I couldn't find her anywhere... or at least not a name that lined up with her age and what I knew she looked like.

I was musing on the conversation I'd had with Josie the night before when my mother walked through the front door of the shop, bringing a strong whiff of White Linen with her.

"Sweetheart! How are you?" She bustled over to me and gave me a hug. "I hope you're not too upset about the other night. I just... wasn't thinking."

"I'm okay," I said, trying not to be irked anymore over my mother's willingness to invite my ex-husband and his new girlfriend to her home, "but Caroline isn't quite as good with it, I'm afraid."

"I kind of picked that up." She grimaced. "Anyway. I heard half the town thinks your friend Denise killed that guy who went off a cliff. What's going on with that?"

"Well, they haven't arrested her," I said. "But I still don't have any idea who actually killed Charles Carsten. Although I have some new leads."

"I heard," she said. "Kirsten told me this morning."

I sighed. "What did she say?"

"She said you two tag-team-interviewed the victim's ex-wife," she said. "Good thing she was there, right?"

I took a deep breath and prepared to respond.

"But the reason I'm here," she said, changing the subject just as I opened my mouth to tell her what I really thought, "is that I was hoping you could point me in the direction of a good cozy mystery. I just finished Louise Penny's latest and I'm looking for a new one."

"Have you read any of Susan Wittig Albert's books yet?" I asked, deciding to run with the subject change. I would deal with my mom's fangirl crush on Kirsten later; I had enough on my plate already. "Laura Childs is also terrific. I love her tea shop mysteries."

"Those sound fun," she said. We spent the next few minutes looking through books; she had selected three and we were walking to the cash register when the upstairs door opened and Winston came hurtling down the steps.

"Mom? Has Winston been out?" Caroline's voice came from the top of the stairs.

"I took him when I got up," I told my daughter. "Your grandma's here, by the way."

"It was so good to see you at the house," my mother said in an overly bright voice.

Caroline grunted.

"I'm so sorry dinner wasn't better for you," my mother continued. "I keep forgetting how weird it must be for you."

"It's fine," Caroline said in a tone of voice that indicated it was anything but. "I'm going back to bed."

"Any interest in driving down to the outlet mall in Freeport later on this week?" my mother asked in a cajoling voice. "I was thinking maybe we could hit the Bean outlet store."

"Maybe," my daughter said, in a way that sounded a lot more like "No." "I'm going to bed now. Bye."

Before my mother could answer, she turned and disappeared into the apartment. I looked down at Winston, who was sitting at my feet looking up at me with merry brown eyes, and petted his head as my mother bit her lip. "That's the first time she's ever refused a trip to the outlet mall," she said.

"She's got a lot going on," I told her. "Kirsten's a lot, actually. And the divorce is hard enough without Kirsten and Ted being attached at the hip."

"Audrey doesn't seem to mind," my mother said, a defensive note in her voice.

"Audrey isn't here," I said.

"Why is Caroline here, anyway? Shouldn't she be in school? She's so bright... if she just applied herself a little bit. I mean, the bookstore gig is fine for a summer job, but it's not really a career."

I sighed. "Can we not have this conversation right now?"

"I didn't mean to say there was anything wrong with you owning a bookstore," my mother said, backpedaling. "But she's got so much talent. Math skills, language skills... She could do anything! I hate to see her throw herself away."

"I'm glad to hear you think so highly of my career choice."

"Oh, Maxine, you know I wasn't talking about you. This is perfect for you. But Caroline... You coddle her," my mother concluded.

"Okay," I said. "How do you propose I get her to go back to school and get reasonable grades? Do we kick her out?"

"Of course not!" my mother objected.

"Then what?"

She shrugged. "I don't know. I'm just the grandma. We didn't have to deal with this with you. You were always such a good student, and we didn't have things like... well, like divorce to deal with."

"That's helpful," I said, feeling the anger I'd suppressed welling up in me. "Are you suggesting Ted and I get back together?"

"Of course not, honey!" She bit her lip. "But you do have to admit that the divorce had... well, it's complicated things."

"That hadn't escaped my notice," I said dryly.

"If only we could find something for Caroline to be passionate about," my mother mused, as if I hadn't been asking myself the same question for months. It must be nice, I reflected, for Ted to be plotting European trips with his new girlfriend while I tried to figure out how to parent a sullen teenager who resisted all attempts to help her start her life. I swallowed back my resentment. In truth, I wouldn't want anyone else to be there for my daughter, and I had faith that she'd find her way. More than anything, I knew, on a deep level she just needed to know she was still loved, even though the family she'd grown up with had splintered apart. It was just frustrating to see my ex jetting off without a care in the world while I wrestled with figuring out how to parent our struggling daughter. And my own mother's fascination with Ted's new literary girlfriend, if I was being dead honest, made me mad. If your own mother isn't on your side, who can you count on?

My mother set the short stack of books on the front desk as she stared into the middle distance, trying to hatch a plot that would light a fire under my daughter. "Maybe she could help you with the marketing?" she suggested, as if the thought had never occurred to me. "I mean, you could obviously use more foot traffic."

I resisted the urge to beat her over the head with one of the paperback cozy mysteries I'd suggested. "That's what she's supposed to be doing," I reminded her. "Remember I told you she was taking over the social media? It's just not happening."

"You can't find a way to motivate her?"

"If I could, she'd be back in school," I said. "But I'm afraid if I sent her back, she'd just flunk out right now. I'm hoping she's just going through a grieving phase and she'll figure it out."

"I still think she needs some tough love," my mother said.

"Well," I said, "I'm open to suggestions. If you think of something, let me know."

"I will," she said. Not that I doubted it. "Do you have time for lunch later this week?"

"Maybe," I said, hearing the same "No" I'd heard in my daughter's voice a few minutes ago. "I've got a lot going on right now."

"I know, but we just haven't seen each other as much as I'd hoped we would."

"I'll see if I have some time," I promised, ringing her up as I spoke. She sailed out of the store a few minutes later, and as the front door swung closed, I heard another door click shut.

Caroline, I realized, had heard our entire conversation.

Fabulous.

18

Bethany came in to cover for me at around three; it was her writing group that night, so I promised I would be back by six and work till close. In the meantime, though, I decided it was time to get out and stretch my legs... besides, Winston needed a walk, too, after all the time sitting on the couch and eating snacks provided by his human sister.

I leashed him up and asked Caroline, who was texting on her phone on the couch, if she wanted to join us.

"Not today," she said.

"I'll see you later, then."

The cliff path passed right behind the house formerly occupied by Charles Carsten... and presumably his son. I still hadn't taken a look at the place where it had all happened, and I could barely feel my ankle injury anymore, so once Bethany took over, I decided it was time for a moody walk along the cliffs. The skies were still leaden, but the fog and rain had been replaced by a cool wind off the water. I grabbed my windbreaker, laced up my boots, and headed to my Kia.

The parking lot for the cliff path was about a half mile down the road from the Carstens' house. I pulled into one of the empty spaces and coaxed my fluffy Bichon out of the Kia.

"I promise, you'll have fun," I told Winston as he eyed me skeptically. Town walks, which might result in a bit of blueberry muffin, were welcome. Wilderness walks without the promise of snacks? Not so much. "Let's go!" I said, and grabbed his round middle gently and lowered him to the pavement. He gave me a resigned look and slowly followed me to the trailhead, sending a wistful glance back at the Kia.

It took a few minutes before he started sniffing the undergrowth. The path wound through a forest whose floor was carpeted with pine needles; on either side of us, trees swayed in the breeze off the water, and the moist air smelled of pine and salt. It was hard to believe the town of Snug Harbor was less than a mile away; the forest felt ancient and primeval, with not a sight or sound of human presence save a few footprints in the soft earth of the trail beneath my feet.

Before long, the canopy of trees gave way to open sky and, below us, the crash of the surf against the rocks at the base of the cliff. I followed the path downward toward the water; for the first time, I saw Charles Carsten's car, which had not yet been towed, where it lay at the bottom of the cliff. I shuddered at the sight of it, and was thankful when the trail dipped back into the trees, away from the crumpled red car.

We were coming closer, though, and as the path wound downward, I caught a whiff of gasoline on the sea-scented air. Before long, we were clambering over the rocks by the shore, just yards away from the upturned car in which Carsten had plunged to his death.

Someone had ringed the area in bright yellow crime

scene tape, but it had torn free in places, and two loose ribbons fluttered in the wind. A seagull lounged on one of the car's crumpled tires, preening its feathers, and already the red finish was dotted with droppings; it didn't take long for nature to start reclaiming things, I thought. The rocks around it were coated in rainbow hues; I was guessing a punctured or collapsed gas tank was responsible for the oily substance, as well as the whiff of gasoline that had wafted up to the trail. I picked my way from the shoreline to the car, the bladderwrack slick and barnacles crunching under my walking boots; the tide was heading out, exposing wet rocks. I don't know why I was drawn to look closer. It might have been morbid curiosity, or a hope that there might be some clue to what had happened tucked into the rocks nearby... maybe something that had sprung free of the car as it hit the ground and escaped the notice of the investigators. I was desperate for anything to free my friend of suspicion. The slick rocks dried as I approached the car, which was on a rise above the high tide line. I kept my distance from the tape, wondering when someone would come to retrieve what remained of Carsten's car. No tow truck was going to be able to make it down here, that was for certain.

I walked around the car. Even though it was upside-down and crumpled, the red finish still gleamed under the seagull droppings, and the creamy leather seats I could see through the shattered windows were unblemished. It had been well tended.

I picked my way around the back of the car, Winston leaping from rock to rock beside me. The trunk latch had come loose in the fall. Something brown poked out of it; it was an accordion folder, I realized as I drew closer to the wrecked vehicle. Glancing around as if I expected the entire Snug Harbor police department to leap out from the beach roses along the cliff edge, I crept toward the fallen car. The seagull eyed me suspiciously as I approached, and a bit of plastic ribbon tickled my cheek as the wind kicked up. Only the corner of the folder was visible, and part of the label: FINAL DOCUMENT.

After one more glance around me, I pulled the sleeve of my jacket down around my fingers to make a makeshift glove; I didn't want to leave fingerprints. I grasped the folder, and as I pulled it out, it tore slightly, releasing several computer printouts onto the barnacle-encrusted rocks.

The seagull let out a startled "caw" and lifted up into the air as I swore under my breath and reached for the pages before the wind could scatter them further. All hope of avoiding leaving fingerprints was lost as I grabbed a page out of the air and stuffed it back into the folder. Once all the pages were together, I picked my way over a few more rocks and sat down on a large granite boulder. Winston leapt up beside me as I settled in and examined the pages that had escaped the brown folder. It appeared to be a will.

How had the police missed this? I wondered as I paged through it. It was dated just last week, and the chief beneficiary was Amanda Duncan, who evidently was to receive the house and the contents of several offshore accounts, along with the yacht in Snug Harbor and the car in whose trunk I had found the document. The only thing transferring to Chad was his father's interest in Venture Investments. I carefully reread the document. Yes, I had understood it right. There was a small bequest to the classic car club, but other than that and what appeared to be a 60% interest in Venture Investments that went to Chad, everything went to Amanda Duncan.

· · ·

I FLIPPED to the last page, looking for a signature, but it was just a series of blank lines, with one for Charles and two for witnesses. Either the will had been executed at the lawyer's office and this was just an unsigned copy, or Charles had never signed it.

Based on Amanda's tearful visit to the bookstore a few days ago, I was guessing he hadn't ever executed it. What was in the first will? I wondered. Had Charles' wife been in line to inherit everything? Had his death happened because Josie realized she was about to be written out of the will and replaced by another woman? Or did she kill him without knowing about it, simply for leaving him and taking up with someone else?

The last name didn't line up, though. Cole. Had Josie kept her maiden name? And even if so, why couldn't I find any reference to her or Charles when I looked for her online?

I put the pages back into the folder and tucked them back into the trunk of the car, peering in as best I could with the phone flashlight to see if anything else was hiding there. All I saw was a set of jumper cables, though, and a few wrenches that gleamed in the light from my phone.

I walked around the car a few times, searching for some other clue, but there was nothing but seagull guano, sun-dried barnacles and a few dried strands of bladderwrack. I even bent down and peered into the car's cabin, steeling myself for what I might find, but aside from a pair of sunglasses and some mints, there was nothing to be found, even in the glove compartment, which had either been searched (doubtful based on my trunk discovery) or had just been forced open by the impact.

It was a relief to leave the car behind, and as I put distance between the crumpled convertible and me, I found myself glancing up at the house on the cliff above. What must have seemed like a safe retreat from the rest of the world had turned out to be the source of Carsten's demise... and one of the things he cherished most the tool that caused it. Money can only do so much, I thought... and as I considered the contents of the will I'd just read, and the tear-streaked face of Amanda in the bookstore the other day, those who wielded it had tremendous power to do harm.

Had money also been the reason he died? I wondered as we left the beach and stepped back into the trees.

As we followed the trail up into the trees, though, Winston suddenly seemed anxious, and not just because we were on a walk. Usually, he would be straining on the leash to get back to the car; now, he was whining and yanking me forward in the other direction.

"What's wrong, buddy?" I asked as he practically pulled me down the path. The further we got, the more agitated he became. I'd never seen him like this before. "Hold on," I said, and moved to switch the leash from my left hand to my right so I could get a better grip. As I was grasping the leash with my right hand, he lunged forward. The leash slithered out of my hand, and the little white dog rocketed down the trail in front of me, his red leash trailing behind him.

"Winston!" I called, but he kept galloping ahead. I ran after him, adrenaline pumping, visions of my little dog lost in the woods, slipping off the rocks into the ocean, hit by a truck as he crossed the highway... "Winston!" I yelled at the top of my lungs, panic gripping me.

He was out of sight, but I could hear him yipping now, from somewhere ahead of me. I ran hard, fueled by adrenaline, leaping over rocks and sliding on the pine-needle-strewn path as my eyes scanned the undergrowth, looking for a patch of white fur. "Winston!" I called again, then gasped at the renewed stab of pain in my ankle as I hurtled down the path, barely avoiding a massive hemlock when the path simultaneously dropped and took a sharp right turn. I swore but didn't stop, feeling my ankle twinge as I ran.

I found my little dog after the next turn on the path. He was standing next to a red jacket, barking as if calling for help. I hustled down the trail, breathing hard and trying to ignore the pain in my ankle, wondering if maybe someone had left treats in the jacket pocket and how they'd managed to forget a jacket on the trail in the first place, when I realized it wasn't just a jacket.

There were jeans poking out from beneath the hem of the jacket, and scuffed white sneakers beneath that. A tumble of brown hair spilled out from beneath the hood.

"Oh, no," I breathed, feeling my heart clench. Winston stopped barking when he saw me. As I hurried over to the prone body, he whined and nudged the hem of the jacket. I gently pulled the hood aside and swept the tumble of brown hair from the neck. As I searched for a pulse with one hand, my other smoothed the hair away from the person's pale face, and I drew in my breath with a start.

It was Amanda Duncan.

19

*A*t the same moment I recognized the young woman, my fingers located a fluttering pulse. I reached for my phone and dialed 911.

"We'll be there as fast as we can," the woman at dispatch said when I told her what I'd found. "Is she breathing?"

I looked down at her still form; as I watched, her chest rose and fell slightly. "She is," I confirmed.

"Any sign of trauma?"

I looked at the red jacket; for the first time I noticed a darker red on the fabric covering her abdomen. "Oh, my God," I breathed. "Yes. There's blood. On the front of her jacket." I pulled the fabric aside to reveal a blood-stained flannel shirt. I pushed it back to discover what looked like a knife wound in her side. "She's been stabbed, on the side of her body. She's bleeding."

"I've got someone coming right now," she said. "Can you raise the wound above her heart?"

"I'll have to roll her over," I said; the wound was on her right side, on the ground.

"I'll stay with you while you do it," she said. As Winston

whined at my side, I rolled Amanda over; it wasn't hard, as she was very slight. The bleeding increased as I moved her, but seemed to subside a bit once I managed to turn her on her side.

"Done," I said.

"How is the bleeding?"

"A little better," I said, watching as a trickle of blood leaked out of the wound, "but still coming."

"Do you have some clean fabric you can use to put on the wound and apply light pressure until the paramedics get there?"

"I do," I said. I tore off my jacket and took off my sweatshirt, which I'd just gotten out of the dryer the day before. I folded it up and pressed it gently to the wound. "I just folded up my sweatshirt and am pressing it against the wound," I said.

"Is that the only place she's bleeding?" the woman on the line asked.

With one hand on the sweatshirt, I pulled the blood-soaked flannel aside and searched for other signs of trauma. "I think this is the only one," I said.

"Good," she said in a calming voice. "Just stay with her and keep applying pressure. They're on their way." As she spoke, I heard the thrum of a helicopter.

Who had stabbed Amanda? And why? The will I'd found wasn't signed; unless there was a fully executed version somewhere, the document giving her Charles's fortune hadn't been put into effect.

And if someone knew she'd found the document—assuming she had, and had used that information to figure out who had killed Charles—why put it back in the car where it would be found by investigators?

Unless this was a random crime with no connection to

what had happened to Amanda. But her location, just yards away from the scene of the first murder, couldn't be coincidence. Could it?

It made no sense at all... and wouldn't, unless Amanda survived her stabbing and could tell us what had happened.

By the time I made it back to the store, it was after five; I had just enough time to grab a quick sandwich before heading down to take over for Bethany. Amanda had been airlifted to the hospital and I had spent at least an hour waiting with Winston for the police to ask me questions. A tired-looking detective asked me a few brief questions. Had I seen anyone, did I know the victim, etc.

"She was... is the girlfriend of the man who died in that accident," I said, nodding toward the car on the beach.

"How do you know that?' she asked.

"It's a small town," I said with a shrug. "Plus, she came into the bookstore just after he died. She was looking for books on contesting wills, and she was upset." I paused. "It made me wonder if maybe this might be connected to what happened to Charles Carsten."

"Maybe," she said. "Hey. Aren't you friends with that barista at Sea Beans?"

"The manager?" I asked. "Denise Wilmington?"

"That's the one," she said. "Do you know where she is today?"

"I... No," I said. "Are you really thinking she might be responsible for this? I mean... what motive would she have?"

"Maybe the girlfriend saw her tampering with the car?" the detective suggested. "I don't know, but if she tells you anything, please get in touch." She handed me her card.

"Have you looked at who stands to inherit?" I asked, thinking of the folder I'd found in the car. "I mean..."

"We are examining all angles," the woman said shortly. "Now, if you hear anything from your friend Denise, let me know, okay?" And with that, she dismissed me.

No wonder Denise was freaking out, I thought as I headed back up the trail with Winston at my heels. I just hoped Amanda was going to come through.

"WHERE DID YOU GO?" Caroline asked, coming into the kitchen with her hair up in a towel turban as I wolfed down the last of my sandwich.

"Somebody stabbed Charles Carsten's girlfriend on the trail behind the Carstens' house," I said. "I found her."

"Oh my God," she said, eyes widening. "Is she... alive?"

"They airlifted her to the hospital," I told her.

"Who did it?"

"I don't know; she was unconscious when I found her." I stood up and put my plate in the dishwasher, then glanced into the little mirror by the front door. "I'm heading downstairs to take over for Bethany."

"Okay," she said. "What's for dinner?"

I stifled a flare of irritation and said, "Whatever's in the fridge. Or you could go to the grocery store."

She sat down on the couch without answering, reaching for the remote control. Winston hopped up beside her and snuggled in, happy to have a couch companion, as thoughts of Amanda briefly receded and I wondered for the hundredth time what to do with my daughter who seemed to have lost her direction... and any desire to find it.

Bethany was already setting up the back room with Devin. "I loved the scene where you found the body," he was saying as I descended the stairs, and a shudder passed through me. I knew Bethany was working on writing a murder mystery, but this evening, it was way too close to home. "I felt like I was there!"

"I didn't go into too much detail?" she asked. "It's a traditional mystery, after all, not a thriller."

"You gave just enough," he said. "The description of the little puddle of blood was perfect."

I sat down behind the desk, feeling a slight wave of nausea, and reflected that art did, in fact, imitate life sometimes. A K.T. Anderson book lay on the desk; I couldn't seem to escape the woman. I picked up the hefty hardcover, with its airbrushed glamor shot of Kirsten on the back, feeling a stab of anger at my ex for being pulled so whole-heartedly into her orbit that he seemed to have forgotten about his children. I opened it and read the blurb on the dust jacket. As usual, there were high stakes and deception and murder... there was murder everywhere, it seemed... only this particular book seemed to hinge on a disappearing media mogul.

Alarm bells rang somewhere deep inside me. Disappearing media mogul. Charles Carsten had almost no history beyond two years ago, and his ex-wife—or wife—had a different name from him. Searches had brought up nothing. The only image I had of any life before Maine was the photo his son had posted on Mother's Day some time ago.

I pulled out my phone and found Chad's Instagram account again. It, too, only dated from two years ago, and there was no mention in recent days of the death of his father... just an image of Snug Harbor from what seemed to be the the bow of the Monkey Business.

I scrolled back through his story until I found the image of Chad with his mother in front of the yacht labeled Happy Hour. As I had noticed before, it looked remarkably like the yacht the Carstens' currently owned... was it possible that Charles had simply painted and renamed it? I switched to Google and searched "yacht registration Happy Hour." It took some doing, but I finally found a vessel that matched the name. A boat built in 1995 came up; I jotted down the VIN number and did another search, ending up on a Coast Guard database. When the owner came up as Charles Kohl, I suddenly realized where I had gone wrong.

Josie's name wasn't Josie Cole.

It was Josie Kohl.

I typed in the name Charles Kohl and pages and pages of results came up. Evidently Charles Kohl had made millions selling fraudulent insurance policies with a company called SafestLife in California; he was so successful he'd even been featured in a Chamber of Commerce profile for Los Angeles County... including a picture of Charles and his then-wife standing beside a familiar red Pontiac Bonneville.

Until someone figured out that what he'd been running was an enormous Ponzi scheme, and a warrant for his arrest was issued.

But the warrant was never served; before anyone could hold Charles to account, he disappeared, leaving his wife alone in their palatial mansion and all of their accounts cleaned out. I wasn't surprised to learn that his son Chad had vanished, too.

Only they hadn't really disappeared. They'd simply

taken on new identities and relocated to the other side of the country.

How had Josie located him? And had she killed her ex-husband... or, rather, her husband... for deserting her, taking their son with him, and starting a relationship with another woman? That would certainly be a viable motive for Amanda's stabbing. If Ted had abandoned me and run off with my children, I know I'd have been tempted. I thought about the meeting the deckhand had described to me. Had she known where he was from the start, or did she only recently find out?

I scrolled through pictures of the formerly happy couple together. They were both glamorous and fashionably dressed, Josie with bleached blond hair and expensive-looking dresses and Charles in a tuxedo or tailored suit, posing at charity balls, being featured in articles on up-and-coming businesspeople... Charles and Josie Kohl had lived a glamorous life in California, all based on Charles Kohl's lies. I had no way of knowing if his wife was in on it, even though she wasn't indicted; evidently the fact that her husband had disappeared with all the money counted in her favor.

I found articles about the victims of his scam, too. People who'd lost their entire life savings because of Charles's actions and been reduced to poverty. A seventy-year-old woman who had put her entire life savings on the line, including getting a mortgage on her home to invest, had lost everything and was now living on the street. Another family had invested in hopes of earning enough money to support their Down's syndrome child after they passed. All gone, and along with it, any hope of their child being cared for after their passing.

And in the meantime, Charles had decamped to Snug Harbor with his million-dollar yacht and bought a cliffside property overlooking the Gulf of Maine with the money his "clients" had scrupulously saved to support basic life functions... and had been conned into handing over to a shyster. Had one of his victims tracked him down and exacted his or her revenge?

I wasn't a fan of murder as a rule, but if someone had to go, I would definitely have put Charles at the top of the list of candidates.

I picked up the phone and pulled out the card the detective who interviewed me on the beach had left me.

She answered on the second ring. "Detective Andrews."

"This is Max Sayers," I said. "I'm the woman you talked to at the crime scene earlier today."

"I remember," she said. "What's up?"

"I have some information for you," I said, and reminded her that the woman I'd found had been the girlfriend of the dead man.

"Yes, you mentioned that," she said in a bored tone of voice.

"I think he was changing his will to make her the beneficiary," I said.

"I'm familiar with the case, and evidently she was not the beneficiary," the detective told me. "How would you know anything about that?"

"I... heard a rumor," I said, not wanting to admit that I was poking around the crime scene. "I also have reason to believe that Charles Carsten used to be Charles Kohl, a conman out of California, and his wife just found him and followed him here."

"Right," she said in a tone of voice that gave me the impression she thought I might be a few cards short of a full deck. "You had quite a shock today, didn't you?" Her voice was compassionate. "Why don't you e-mail me what you've, uh, discovered, and we'll take it from there?"

"Look up Charles Kohl," I said, spelling out the last name. "His ex-wife... or wife... is Josie Kohl, and she's staying at the Snug Harbor Inn."

"How did you come by that information?" she asked.

"The deckhand of the Carstens' yacht told me a woman named Josie Kohl visited him onboard last week, and I tracked her down to the inn. And then I googled her and figured out who Charles Carsten really was. I mean, I figured it out through his wife's name."

"Right. What's the deckhand's name?"

"I... I don't remember. I'm not sure she told me."

"Okay. Well, um, e-mail everything to me, and I'll be sure to look into it," she said in a tone of voice that was decidedly unenthusiastic.

"I'm not making this up," I said. "I'm worried Josie Kohl killed Charles Carsten, formerly Kohl, and then went after his girlfriend, all because her husband abandoned her."

"Right," she said again. "I promise to look into it. Now, why don't you go get some rest, maybe call a friend?"

"Fine," I said. "But please let me know what you find out."

"I still have your number," she said. "Now go find someone to spend the evening with."

I hung up, feeling completely invalidated... and afraid that Charles Carsten's killer was not just free, but free to go after Amanda and make sure the job was done.

If only she would wake up and be able to identify her would-be killer...

Until she did, though, there was a murderer on the loose. And it didn't look like the detective in charge of the case was in any hurry to find out who that was.

20

I normally don't close the store before the official closing time, but Caroline was nowhere to be found and Bethany was busy with her mystery group.

"I've got an errand to do," I told her, interrupting the critique for a moment so I could let her know I was closing up shop. The place was pretty dead, anyway, so I wasn't horribly worried about losing business. "I'll be back as soon as I can."

"Where are you going?"

"The Snug Harbor Inn," I said, and when a little line of puzzlement appeared between her eyebrows, I added, "I'll explain later. But if I'm not back by close, please call this number." I jotted down the detective's number and handed it to her.

"Okay," she said. "Are you sure this is a good idea?"

"I'll be fine," I said. "And if I'm not back or haven't called, just call the number and tell her what I said." I hoped that would be enough to stir her to come find me.

"Have fun!" I added in a cheery voice as the four writers blinked up at me. Devin, I noticed, was only an inch or two away from Bethany, and the two were leaning toward each other. I smiled to see it, then turned and headed to turn the sign on the front door to CLOSED and locked it.

The sun was dropping low in the sky as I pulled out of the driveway behind Seaside Cottage Books. I dialed Nicholas on the phone, putting it on the car speaker as I headed toward the Snug Harbor Inn. Unfortunately, I got voicemail, so I left a brief message outlining my thoughts and what I planned to do, and then hung up, wondering if I was being a total idiot.

My anxiety rose as I drove, and by the time I reached the grand old building, my chest was tight and my palms were sweating. I turned off the car and hurried into the inn; first I scanned the bar and restaurant, but there was no sign of Josie. I jogged back to the front desk. "Can you call Josie Kohl's room for me?" I asked.

"Sure, but she just left a few minutes ago," the manager said. "Can I leave her a message?"

"Did she say where she was going?"

"She asked the quickest way to get to the harbor," he said.

The harbor. Which meant she was going to the Monkey Business... to confront her son? Would she kill him, too?

"How long ago?"

"Only a few minutes," he said. "She looked a little agitated, now that I think of it."

"Thanks," I said, and as I hurried back to the entrance, he called to me.

"Are you sure you don't want me to leave a message?"

"I do," I said. "If Nicholas Waters calls asking for Max Sayers tell him I'm at the Monkey Business on the pier."

~

I MADE it to the harbor in record time, and found a spot at the far end of the parking lot. Nicholas hadn't called back, so I texted him what I was doing and where I was going, just in case something went wrong. I got out of the car, shoved the phone into my back pocket, and hurried toward the dock, wondering, yet again, if I was worrying for nothing. I was almost sure Josie Kohl had killed Charles Carsten and attacked his girlfriend. Why was she on the Monkey Business? Would she kill her son, too?

As I stepped onto the dock, relieved to see the Monkey Business was still there, a boat engine started. To my horror, I realized it was the Monkey Business. I hurried over to the yacht... the deckhand I'd talked with the other day was there, tending the ropes.

"Is Josie Kohl here?" I asked.

She nodded. "How did you know?"

"I think she killed your boss," I said. "And tried to kill his girlfriend."

Her eyes bulged. "Seriously?"

"Seriously," I said. "Can I come aboard?"

"I'm not supposed to..." She glanced up toward the wheelhouse. The captain was distracted, talking to someone behind him. "Yes," she said decisively, reaching out a hand and letting me hop aboard. "You can't say I let you on, though... and stand where he can't see you." She motioned me to scuttle along the side of the boat, out of sight of the captain. "What are you going to do?" she asked as the order to cast off came over her radio.

"Find Josie and make sure she doesn't do in Chad," I said.

"He's driving the boat," she said as she loosened the ropes.

"Who is?"

"Chad," she said. "He fired the captain today."

"So who's the crew?"

"It's just me right now," she said, racing to the back of the boat to release the lines. "Which is weird." She undid the rope from the cleat, pushing off as Chad gunned the engine and the yacht pulled out of its berth. "You really think she killed him?" she asked.

"We'll find out," I said, taking a deep breath and heading toward the back of the boat.

The yacht looked like something out of a television show, with brass rails and teak everything, all shined to perfection. I took a deep breath as I put my hand on the polished brass knob to the interior. I was totally trespassing, and had no idea what the consequences were, legally. But if I could prevent a murder...

The first room was a living room of sorts, with a big sectional couch and gorgeous views out every window. It was empty, with two choices; I could go up in the direction of the wheelhouse, or follow a staircase down. My instinct told me to move away from the main area, so I went down, and entered a small hallway. There were two doors; the first, on the right, led to a bedroom with two twin beds. It was empty. I opened the one on the left to find a matching room, but with a rumpled bed... and an anxious-looking Josie Kohl standing at the window, looking out at the receding shoreline.

She turned at the sound of the door opening and did a double-take. "What are you doing here?"

"I know about your husband," I said.

"What? What about him?"

"He went over that cliff a few days after you tracked him down," I said. "I can understand you being angry with him. But why Amanda?"

"I'm sorry," she said, a groove between her eyebrows. "What are you talking about?"

"Amanda Duncan," I repeated. "You stabbed her on the beach by the accident. Were you jealous? Did you think she'd taken all of the money that was coming to you?"

"Oh, God," she said, paling. "Is she okay?"

"I don't know. She's unconscious, in the hospital."

A look of pain crossed her features, and I suddenly realized I had it all wrong. "It wasn't you," I said. "It was your son, wasn't it?"

"No," she said weakly. "He's a good boy. He had his moments, but he'd never hurt anyone." I could see the lie in her eyes; she wanted to believe it, but she didn't.

"Why did he kill his father?" I asked, then thought of the will I'd found in the car. The one that hadn't been executed. "He knew he was planning to write him out of the will, didn't he?"

"Charles was never supportive of Chad," Josie said. "All Chad wanted to do was prove himself to his father. But Charles was too controlling."

"So Chad cut the brake lines of his car."

"It was an accident," Josie said weakly. "Chad would never do something like that."

"He deserved it," said a voice from behind me. I turned to see Chad Carsten. "Who let you on?"

"I... I snuck on," I said. "Amanda is still alive, you know."

A look of dismay crossed his features. "What? How do you know about that?"

"You didn't," his mother moaned.

"I did what I had to," Chad said, the words tumbling out. "She was going to take everything. I had to protect us."

21

"Not us. He left me long ago," Josie said, her voice thick with grief. "You... you killed your father?" she said.

"Like you just said, he abandoned you," Chad said. "He was going to disinherit me. He was keeping me from being my own man, and was going to hand everything over to that... that bitch," he said, and his chin thrust out. "I couldn't let that happen. I had a perfectly good business model, and my supportive, loving father just completely tanked it. Just like always." I could hear the hurt under the sneer in his voice.

"The coffee house chain?" I asked.

"The coffee house chain," he confirmed. "He couldn't even back me on that. He told me he was going to pull the funding, forcing me to sell the ones we already invested in, and cut me out of the will."

"Why would he do that?"

"He said I had to learn to make my own way, and that what I was doing was too risky. Like frickin' defrauding half of California wasn't risky. I had a good scheme going; he just couldn't admit it because he didn't come up with it himself."

"What was the scheme?"

"I was going to use the coffee houses to... process money," he said.

"Process money? What money?" his mother asked, speaking for the first time since her son had admitted killing her ex-husband.

"I have a sideline I've developed," Chad said. "With one of the partners at Venture Investments. We just need a solid set of businesses on the coast to help us with the funding."

"So you weren't really in it to make money selling coffee," I said. "What was the sideline?"

"It's lucrative, that's all I'll say," he said with a quirked smile. "We're going to pick up a drop right now, since you mention it. Although I might have to drop you off, too," he said, giving me a hard look. "And then make a trip back to the hospital."

"Did she see you?" Josie asked. "If she wakes up, will she be able to identify you?"

"Amanda? I don't think so. I came up behind her."

"How did you find out he was going to leave his money to her?" I asked, thinking of the will in the folder I'd found.

"I already told you. He said it right to my face," Chad said bitterly. "Said he decided he was keeping me back by just giving me what he'd earned. Then he said he couldn't take the risk of doing anything that could bring scrutiny on the family, so he put the kibosh on my business venture. He was going to leave me penniless and jobless."

"He said he was leaving his money to Amanda Duncan?"

"He didn't tell me that, but I found a copy of his new will when I broke into his computer. And he had an appointment with an attorney coming up."

"So you cut the brake lines before he could change it."

"What else was I supposed to do? I was about to lose my inheritance to that jumped-up piece of trash. Her and that broke-ass brother. He was the one who put her up to it."

"Her brother?" I asked.

"Oh, yeah. Hanging around all the time. He was living off of her... living off my dad."

I remembered the conversation I'd seen at the Salty Dog, between Amanda and a young man named John. "Did they have the same last name?"

"No, they had different fathers. Why?"

"I think I saw them the other day, is all."

"Of course you did. He followed her everywhere. Put up her dating profile and everything... she was his cash cow."

"You didn't have to kill him," his mother said, turning the subject back to where we started. "We could have talked. Why did you leave me in California? I've never understood that. I tried so hard to be there for you..." Her eyes welled with tears.

"Of course you loved me," he said. "I love you, too... you're the best mom ever. And now that all of what should have been ours is mine, we can go back to how things were. How they should have been."

"But that money's not ours," she said. "He stole it."

"No one will know unless we tell them," he said, and his eyes turned to me.

"No," Josie said. "You're not a killer, Chad. You committed a crime of passion, you felt abandoned by your dad." Her voice was urgent, pleading. Scared. "You're not a killer," she repeated.

I was not convinced. A cold tingle ran down my spine, and my eyes began searching the room for potential weapons. Unless I could find some way to grab a pillow and suffocate him, though, I was out of luck; even the lamps were attached to the walls. Another downside of boats.

"I'm protecting us," he said in a cajoling tone. As he spoke, he reached into his pocket and pulled out what looked like a very large Swiss Army knife. He did something, and a big blade sprang out. "Mom, we can talk about this more, but I need you to tie her up now."

"Tie her up?" Josie said, blinking at him. "You're kidding me, right?"

"Mom," he said. "We have a way to be together. Without him. He won't hurt you again."

"He didn't mean to," Josie said. "He just got angry sometimes. He was never taught to control it."

"He hurt both of us," Chad said. "He loved those cars more than us; you know it's true. So he got to die in one."

"Chad," she said. "You don't have to do this. We can get you help..."

"Are you with me?" He asked her in an eerie voice that made a shiver run down my spine. "I have to have you with me. I did all of this for both of us."

"Chad..."

"Don't move," he said. "I'll be back with rope. Mom," he said, looking at a pale-faced Josie, "I'm trusting you."

He stepped out of the room, staring at her, and closed it behind him. I heard a bolt snick shut.

"I'm so sorry," Josie said, tears springing from her eyes and her shoulders slumping as the door shut.

"Never mind that," I said, pulling my phone out of my pocket. No signal; we must be out of range. "We have to get out of here. Find some way to call for help. Is your phone working?"

She pulled her phone out. "Nothing," she said, then moaned as I ran to the door and turned the knob. Hope flared briefly, then died as I pulled and pushed to no avail. "I can't believe my son is doing this. He's not himself... he's really a sweet boy," she said. "It must be some medication he's on..."

"Look," I said, scanning the room for something to use to defend myself. "If I can't find a..." I stopped myself, realizing she wasn't going to be on board with me braining her son. "What I mean is, he's going to be back with rope. If you have to tie me up, make it so I can get out, okay?"

"I can't tie you up," she said.

"If he does it, I'll never get out and I won't be able to help you."

"You won't turn him in, will you?" she asked. "He needs help. We have to get him help."

"Of course he needs help," I said. "But if he does something horrible, it's going to make it harder. And you don't want blood on your hands. Or his."

"He already has blood on his hands," she said, burying her head in her hands.

"He needs help," I reiterated. "Just focus on getting him help." As she sat on the bed sobbing, I hurried into the bathroom and pulled the cabinets open, searching for something. The only useful thing I could find was hairspray; if nothing else, it might blind him if I sprayed it in his face? I set it on the counter and kept pulling things open, looking for something I could use. Shampoo, hair dryer, soap, towels... I was coming up empty.

"He's coming back," Josie moaned from the bed. I grabbed the hairspray and hurried out of the bathroom just as the knob turned. I had enough time to shove the can under a pillow before he was shutting the door behind him and handing the rope to his sobbing mother.

"Do it," he said, staring at me, the knife in his right hand.

"Is that what you stabbed Amanda with?" I asked, having the odd thought that it wasn't very hygienic to use the same knife without sterilizing it, before reminding myself that the point of using the knife was to kill people, so avoiding infection wasn't a big priority.

"I don't know why it matters, but it is," he said, glancing down at the knife as his mother stood, holding the coil of rope with drooping shoulders and looking sick. "It was a gift from my father for my 21st birthday. She got a ring for her birthday, with a five-carat diamond. I got a pocket knife."

"Big pocket knife," I observed.

"Not big enough if Amanda is still breathing," he noted, then turned to his mother. "Tie her up."

"Chad..."

I gave her a hard glance, and our eyes met briefly.

"Do it," he repeated, a menacing edge to his voice, and she knelt at my feet and began wrapping the rope around my ankles. Too loosely, though. "Tighter than that," he ordered, reaching down and yanking the rope so that it bit into my ankle.

"Ouch," I said, wincing involuntarily. She wrapped it around another five or six times, and then he bent down to cut the rope.

"Knot it hard," he instructed her. I tried to pull my ankles apart a little as she fumbled with the rope, to create a little bit of slack, but it was too late. I'd have to do that earlier with my hands... if I was able to do it without him noticing. She finished up the knot, and he gave it a tug. "Not perfect, but it will do for now," he said. She stood up. "Now her hands. Put them behind your back," he instructed me, and I did so, then turned my body toward her.

The rope was rough against my wrists, and once the first loop was done, I pulled my hands apart a bit, hoping he wouldn't notice. It might not be enough, but it was something.

He didn't say anything, and I pulled harder as more loops encircled my wrists, creating a gap that I hoped I'd be able to take advantage of.

"Good," he said, finally, and then, "I'll tie it."

"No," she said, and I could hear a whisper of maternal authority in her voice. "I'll finish it."

I could feel her fingers working, then there was a final tug, and she said, "There. That will hold her. Now," she said, sounding like a different woman than she had a few minutes ago. "Tell me about this drop."

"I'm not sure I should," he said. "You might not like it."

"I've been thinking about it," she said, her shoulders still slumped. "Your father did hold you back. I'm glad to see you taking charge, doing things on your own, not just taking what he gave you. He may not have supported you, but I want to." I heard a quiver in her voice as she spoke.

"Oh, Mom," he said. "I hoped you'd understand. You really support me?" He sounded younger, and I could hear the hurt and rejection he must have experienced at the hands of his father as he spoke.

"I always support you, Chad," she said, and I could hear both sadness and tenderness as she spoke. "You're my son. I love you."

"Thank you," he said, and his voice was raw. "I love you too. Here... let me show you what I have planned," he said. "I met this guy about six months ago," he was beginning as they walked out of the bedroom and shut the door behind them. As their footsteps retreated, I found myself wondering if Josie really had decided to support her son in his murderous endeavors, or if she was just a really, really good actress.

But I didn't plan to wait around and find out.

22

*S*he'd tied me tighter than I'd hoped. The legs were impossible, but I'd managed to leave a little play between my wrists. I wriggled and pulled my wrists apart, trying to loosen the rope further and wishing he'd used something a little less rough; I had already rubbed the skin raw. I pulled and pulled and twisted... eventually, I felt a little bit of play. I reached over and hooked the loose bit over one of the knobs of the night stand, jamming the drawer shut with my knee, and pulled toward me. One of the loops was sliding up my wrists toward my hands. I gritted my teeth and pulled harder, ignoring the fiery pain as the rope tore at my skin. Finally, on the fourth try, the rope sprang off. I unraveled the rest of it and then went to work on my ankles. It wasn't long before I was free... except for the fact that I was stuck on a boat with no cell phone access and nobody knew where I was.

The first thing I did was check the door. It was, of course, locked. I turned and looked out the windows; the coastline was receding fast. My phone still had no bars; even if Nicholas got the text and found out where I had gone, the

Monkey Business was heading to open water. I was completely on my own, with nothing but a can of Vidal Sassoon hair spray to defend me.

How had I gotten it so wrong? I wondered. And what exactly was Chad's endeavor that his father thought it was going to draw too much attention... and why did it require what sounded like money laundering?

Unfortunately, it looked like I was about to find out.

The time ticked by, and Chad and Josie didn't return. I sat down on the bed, reflecting that I'd often wondered what it was like inside a yacht, but that in truth I'd rather be just about anywhere but this expensively decorated master bedroom on water. I peered out the window; we were turning now. Where were we going? As I watched, we approached an island I recognized; it had a lighthouse on the point. We soon passed it, though, and I watched as the tall spire disappeared behind a stand of dark green trees.

It must have been a half hour, during which I obsessively checked my phone for signal (there was none), but it felt like a day before the engine changed timbre and the boat slowed. Adrenaline shot through me, and I grabbed the can of hairspray and inched toward the door.

Outside the window, I saw a rocky coastline go by, and then a long wooden dock that looked like it had seen better days. The boat reversed slightly, and I heard a radio outside the window and footsteps overhead.

It took a few minutes, but I heard what I'd been waiting for; the sound of footsteps down the stairs outside the door. I grabbed my can of hairspray tight, and when the door opened, I held it out and hit the nozzle.

"Ouch! My eyes!"

It was the deckhand.

"I'm so sorry," I said as she blundered into the room, her

hands covering her eyes. "What are you doing down here?" I glanced behind her, into the hallway; no one was there.

"I was just coming to get my hat," she said. "What are you doing spraying hairspray at me?"

"I thought you were your boss."

"Why spray him?"

"It's your boss who's the murderer, not his mother," I whispered.

She blinked at me. "What?"

"They tied me up. He killed his dad. I think they're going to kill me."

"Oh my God. Really?"

"I swear!" I said. "Look... here are the ropes. And my wrists are all messed up... look." I showed her my reddened wrists. She squinted at them through swollen eyes.

"You're serious, aren't you?"

"Dead serious," I said. "Although I'm hoping not to be dead."

"I've been working for a murderer?" she said.

"I'm afraid so," I said. "So we have to think about what to do next."

"I don't really want to think. I just want to get off this boat."

"You and me both" I said. "Do you have a way to reach the mainland?"

"I have the radio," she said. "But they'll probably hear me. I'll have to be sneaky."

"Where are we?"

"Porcupine Island," she said.

"Are there any houses on the island?"

She shook her head. "Too steep. Too small."

"Why are we here, anyway?"

"I don't know," she said. "There's another boat here,

though... a small one. Chad got out and is talking to them. I thought it was one of his friends."

"Where's Josie?"

"Drinking a martini in the bar."

"Let's go then," I said.

"Go and do what?"

"Get out of here while he's off the boat," I said.

"Oh. Of course. That makes sense."

"I'll untie the ropes and you get the engine going."

She bit her lip. "I'll lose my job."

"Your boss tied me up and murdered his father," I pointed out. "Do you really want this job?"

"Good point," she said. "Hey. Maybe a write-up for heroism could help get me a promotion with another yacht."

"Think that way," I said. "What's your name, by the way?"

"Jessica," she said.

"I'm Max," I told her. "Now go, Jessica. I'll untie the ropes... you steer the boat."

"Are you sure?"

"What other option do we have?" I asked.

"Right," she said, and together we hurried up the stairs.

"I'll go untie the ropes," I told her. "Get ready to go; but don't start the engine until we're loose."

"Got it," she said. "Are you sure?"

"Positive," I said. "Let's go."

As she bounded up the stairs to the wheelhouse, I crouched down and let myself out the door to the back deck. Chad was deep in conversation with another young man on the dock; the other man was clutching a duffel bag. I crept to the closest cleat and began unwinding the rope.

"How much?" Chad asked.

"Fifty thousand," the other man responded. "We'll have another fifty the day after tomorrow. When can you handle more?"

"We'll be open here in a few weeks," Chad said. "That means we can do another twenty percent, and we're still growing."

"Great," the man said. "Sorry about your old man," he continued as I finished untying the rope and crept to the front of the yacht. "I hear some local did him in."

"Yeah," Chad said. "Cray-cray lady. They haven't arrested her yet, but it's coming."

I got to the second cleat as they spoke, and was had almost finished untying it when a voice came from behind me.

"What are you doing? How did you get out?"

I whirled to see Josie, a martini in hand, standing a few feet behind me on the deck.

"Hey!" Chad called from the dock, and started running toward the yacht.

I yanked the rope off the cleat and yelled, "Go! Go! Go!"

The engine sputtered. The man with the bag took a step toward me; at the same time, Chad reached for the railing, about to board. Just in time, the engine caught and Jessica pulled away from the dock. Chad, one leg on and one leg off, stretched, then fell into the water as the Monkey Business picked up speed.

"What are you doing?" Josie asked, frantic. "You can't leave him here."

"Josie," I said, "he was probably going to kill me. I thought you were on my side!"

"Blood is thicker than water," she said. "Besides, he did it for me. Charles was a jerk... he defrauded all of those people and abandoned me. We're going back to get him."

"No," I said. "We're going back to shore and calling the authorities."

"We're not," she said. She turned and walked down the deck.

"Where are you going?" I asked as she put her drink down on the bar and reached under the counter. And then I was looking at the wrong end of a gun.

23

"We're going back," she repeated.

"Where did that come from?"

"Charles was paranoid. He had these things stashed everywhere. Now, let's go." She waved me toward the stairs, following me as I headed up to the wheelhouse.

"This isn't going to make it better," I said. "He's probably going to kill me. And you'll be accessory to murder. This just makes it all worse."

"I can't abandon my son," she said. "A mother never abandons her child."

"He killed his father," I pointed out. "What's to say he won't kill you? And are you okay with that young woman dying, too? She's totally innocent. She's somebody's daughter."

"Just... just go," she said. "Stop talking."

I got to the top of the stairs; there was a short hallway, and a door with a window into the wheelhouse. I could see the back of Jessica's head, her long hair pulled back in a ponytail. She was so young. Was she going to die because she had let me onto the boat? She was almost the same age as my daughters. My heart contracted. Would I ever see them again? Would they even know what happened to me?

"Are you sure you want to do this?" I asked.

"Yes," she said.

"He left you. He went with his father. Besides, how will you defend him if you're in jail, too?"

"We're not going to jail," she said. "I've been apart from him for two years already. I'm not going to give him up again. Now, go."

She gave me a shove, and I could feel the barrel of the gun pressing against my back. I opened the door. "Everything okay?" Jessica asked as she turned around. When she saw Josie behind me, her eyes widened. They were still swollen and red from the hairspray. "What's she doing behind you?"

"She's got a gun," I said.

"I want you to go back and get my son," she announced.

"He's already right behind us," she said. "They're following us back."

"Then slow down and let him board," she said.

"He's not alone," Jessica pointed out. "He's with some shady-looking guy."

"Let him board," she repeated.

Jessica gave a slight shrug. "Okay. But I think that guy's bad news." As Josie continued to press the barrel of the gun to my back, she pulled back on the throttle. Soon, the engine was idling and I could feel the yacht slowing to a stop, the waves beneath the boat rocking us gently.

"Let's go," Josie said, and Jessica led the way as we headed to the back of the yacht, where Chad and his buddy, who were in a speedboat, were already cutting in. Chad was driving, and his friend held a rope in one hand and a gun in the other. A big gun.

"Told you," Jessica said, and the calmness of her voice impressed me. She would be a good captain someday. Or would have been. I couldn't see how both of us wouldn't end up dead.

"Who are these people?" the guy with the gun barked as the smaller boat idled. He couldn't tie up the boat without two hands, I realized, and Chad was busy trying to keep the boat lined up with the back of the yacht. "I thought you came alone except for the chick driving the boat."

"This is my mother," Chad babbled. "She's with us. The woman with her is a stowaway... she's nosy."

"Your mother?" the man said in disbelief. "Why the hell is she here?"

"She came to visit just before I was due to meet you," he said. "I told her to stay below deck."

"You're sloppy," he said. "My boss warned me that you were an amateur."

"Don't talk to my son that way," Josie said from behind me, and I felt the gun leave the small of my back. I turned to see her pointing it at the angry-looking man in the speedboat.

"Whoa," he said, moving the gun so it pointed not at me, but at Josie's son. "Kill me and you take out your boy, too."

"What?" Chad said. "We're partners."

"Business partners," the man clarified. "And you're not holding up your end of the bargain."

"I did everything you said," Chad said. "I handle the money. I'm expanding our capacity. I even took care of my father."

"You don't need this man," Josie said from behind me. "With everything your father left you, you don't need to get involved in this. We can just leave him his money and walk away."

"Says who?" the man replied. His eyes were flat and calculating and scared the bejeezus out of me. "I didn't say he could walk away. We have an agreement."

"We'll pay you," Josie said. "Five hundred thousand dollars. If you let us walk away. Right, Chad?" she added, and I could hear desperation in the high pitch of her voice.

"Five hundred thousand is a good start," the man said. "But we need to take care of the witnesses." He redirected the gun toward me and cocked it.

Oh, God. "Do you really want blood all over the boat?" I blurted, moving my body instinctively to shield Jessica. "We should go somewhere else."

He paused, considering. "You have a point. Get in the boat," he ordered.

"We're not anchored," Jessica reminded him. "Do you really want to leave the Monkey Business unattended?"

The man swore, then turned to Chad. "No wonder your old man didn't think you could hack it. You really are an incompetent ass. Maybe I should just kill you, too."

As he said those words, I heard an explosion from behind me. A look of shock flashed across the man's face, and then a bloodstain blossomed on the front of his jacket, and he crumpled to the floor of the boat.

"Mom," Chad said in a little-boy voice. "What have you done?"

"He was going to kill you, Chad," she said. "I was protecting you."

"Crap," he said, running a hand through his hair. "What do we do now?"

"We leave," she said. "We take on other identities."

"What about these two?" he asked, looking at Jessica and me. "I don't... I don't want more blood on my hands."

"We leave them on the island," she said. "Then we take

the money out of the bank, rename the yacht, and disappear."

"There is no money yet, Mom," he said. "We have to wait for probate to finish."

"You think they're not going to ask where that money came from? They'll figure out who your father was, or why his brake lines were cut, and all of it will be gone and you'll be in jail. No. I think we take the fifty thousand or whatever's in that bag, leave these two on an island somewhere, and head to Mexico or something. We can sell the yacht and live on what we make. It's worth a million, right? Maybe two? That will take us a long way."

"You'd walk away from everything?" he asked, blinking

"You walked away," she said. "Why can't we? And then we can be together. And leave all of this behind us."

"What if someone finds them?"

"We'll take their phones. We'll be long gone by the time they get found... if they get found... and there will be no more blood on our hands. I don't like killing. Now. Does anyone else ever go to that island you were talking about?"

"I've never seen anyone there," he said. "There used to be a house that went with the dock, but it's been deserted for years."

"Then we'll leave them there," she said. "And we'll head out to open water and figure out what to do from there."

"What about the speedboat?"

"We'll throw what's-his-name's body over, wipe it down, and let it drift. It's not our problem. All right," she said, turning the gun on Jessica and me. "You two. Downstairs again."

"I'll tie up the boat while you take care of them," Chad said.

"And then we'll be off," she said. "Come on," she said,

and followed us into the yacht and down the stairs to the lower staterooms. "Give me your phones," she said, and we surrendered them to her. A moment later, the door shut behind us, and we were alone.

"I'm so sorry about all of this," I said to Jessica after the door lock snicked shut.

"Don't be," she said, and pulled what looked like a green walkie talkie out of her jacket pocket.

"What's that?" I asked.

"An emergency beacon," she said in whisper. "I grabbed it and activated it as soon as I saw the gun."

"Oh my God. You mean the coast guard knows where we are?"

"I imagine so. The only downside is that they're probably trying to hail us on the radio," she said. "I turned mine off and shoved it in my pocket. I'm hoping they're distracted enough by cleaning out the speedboat that they don't hear the radio in the wheelhouse." She turned her radio on as we spoke, fiddled with the dials, and spoke into it.

"Monkey Business to Coast Guard." She paused, and a moment later, the radio crackled to life.

"Coast Guard, go ahead," a woman's voice said.

"Last known location was Porcupine Island, heading out to sea," she said. "We're locked in one of the lower staterooms. The two people manning the boat are armed and dangerous. Going to radio silence. Over and out."

"Ten-four," came the response. Jessica turned off the radio and tucked it back into her pocket, along with the beacon.

"In case they overheard me or come looking for it," she explained.

"You are amazing," I told her. "You're going to make an incredible captain someday."

"If we live that long," she said, but she couldn't help but smile.

A moment later, the engine started up again and the boat turned around, back toward the island with the rickety dock.

"I hate that island. It's got a bad reputation. At least the Coast Guard will have a way to find us," she said.

"What do we do if they get here before we reach the island?" I asked.

"You know, that's a good point. I think we should bar the door from the inside, just in case they decide they want to hold us hostage or something," she suggested.

"Bar it with what? There's no loose furniture."

"We can tie that rope from the handle to the bed," she suggested.

"It's flush to the floor with nothing to tie it to," I said. "Let's tie it to the bathroom doorknob instead."

"Good call."

I picked up the longest piece of rope and handed it to her; within minutes, she had a taut line between the knobs. It might be locked from the outside, but now, at least, we could control who entered as well.

No sooner had she finished testing her last knot than a distant, rhythmic thrumming noise sounded. "Is that what I think it is?" I asked as the sound got closer.

She peered through the window and fist-pumped the air. "It's a helicopter," she said. "And it's heading our way."

∼

THE BOAT SLOWED A MOMENT LATER, and then the engine stopped. We heard the helicopter for several minutes; then there was another sound, of a boat engine.

"A cutter," Jessica announced from her spot at the window. "I think they're going to board."

"I hope Chad and his mother don't do anything stupid," I said. As I spoke, footsteps thundered down the steps and then the hallway.

"We should get down," I whispered. "Just in case." As we dropped to the floor, the lock snicked and the doorknob rattled. The door didn't budge, though. Chad's voice sounded from the hallway. "Open up!"

Jessica grabbed my hand, and we remained silent as he pounded on the door and swore. Then the door shuddered as he kicked it. On the third kick, the wood cracked. But before he could kick it a fourth time, a woman's voice sounded. "What's in there?"

"I... I don't know," the man said. "The door is jammed."

"Drop your weapon," the woman ordered. I heard a thud, and a moment later, I heard her voice on the other side of the door. "Coast guard. Anyone in there?"

"Yes," Jessica called out. "I'm the one who activated the beacon."

Chad said, "Beacon? What beacon?"

"We received a distress call from this vessel," the woman said. "Please stand back."

It took only moments for Jessica to undo the rope and open the door.

"Thank you so much for coming," I said.

"Are you okay?" the woman asked.

"We're fine now," I said.

"How many people are there we should know about?" she asked.

"This guy and a woman," Jessica said. "He's my former boss. He killed someone on the mainland, and his mother—the woman—killed another man just a few minutes ago."

"I didn't kill anyone!" Chad protested, looking like a scared three-year-old

"Killed him?" the coast guard officer asked. "How?"

"She shot him," I said. "He was on a speedboat. They pushed him overboard and let the boat go after wiping their prints."

"Why?" she asked.

"I think it was a money-laundering operation that went south."

"That was the cause of both murders?"

"The other was a family affair," I said.

"Sounds like some family," she said.

"Oh, they are," Jessica said. "I worked for them for the past six months."

The coast guard officer looked at her with interest. "You handled today well. Have you considered joining the Coast Guard instead of being a yachtie?"

"I hadn't, but after this experience? I'm seriously considering it," Jessica said, shaking her head and eyeing Chad, who looked like a cornered rat in topsiders. "I think it might be safer."

24

*N*icholas was waiting for me at the dock when we moored in the berth the Monkey Business had occupied all summer, accompanied by the Coast Guard vessel. Thankfully, so were the Snug Harbor police.

"Oh, thank God," he said as I emerged from below deck; I'd never seen him looking so pale.

I clambered over the railing and jumped onto the pier and into his arms.

"I thought you were gone," His voice was rough with emotion. "You left me that message and then you weren't answering the phone and then I got here and the Monkey Business was gone, and then the police came... What the hell happened?"

"I figured out who murdered Charles Carsten," I said as the police cuffed both Chad and his mother. "Or at least I thought I did. I thought it was Josie, but it turned out to be his son."

"Why are they arresting his mother? Was she an accessory?"

"No," I said. "She killed her son's crime-gang partner."

"His what?"

"It's a long story," I said, hugging him. "I don't even know all of it. But I'm okay, the murderer is in cuffs, and Denise is off the hook." My mind turned to Amanda, who had been unconscious in the hospital a few hours ago. "I need to make a phone call," I said, and then realized my phone was still in the yacht somewhere. Or the water... I didn't know what had happened to it. "Can I borrow your phone?"

"Of course," he said. I googled the Snug Harbor Hospital and called, asking if I could speak with Amanda Duncan, hoping against hope she might be awake. They put me through, and a weak-sounding young woman's voice answered.

"Is this Amanda Duncan?" I asked.

"It is," she said.

"Thank God."

"Who is this?" she asked.

"Max Sayers," I said.

"Who?"

"We met at the bookstore. I'm the one who found you," I said. "Do you remember what happened?"

"Somebody attacked me," she said.

"He's in custody now," I said.

"What? How do you know?"

"He confessed to it," I said.

"How do you know all of this?"

"It's a long story... I'll tell you when I visit."

"It was Chad, wasn't it?" she asked.

"It was. How did you know?"

"He was upset because Charles wouldn't fund his coffee shop venture anymore... and because he was changing his will. Chad... Chad killed him before he could get it signed and witnessed."

"Did you put that will in the back of the car? After it

went over the cliff?"

"I did," she said. "That was why I was down there. I didn't think the police would believe me if it came from me, so I thought if they found it..."

"How did Chad know you were onto him?"

"I told him I thought he'd done it," she said. "He saw me in his dad's office the other day, looking through papers. He told me to leave... that I wasn't welcome in the house anymore." She sighed. "I'd already found the will, and it was in my bag. I was angry, so I told him I thought he'd killed his dad for money. He was furious."

"Because you were right," I said. "I'm just glad you're alive."

"Me too," she said.

"Is your brother there?"

"My brother? How do you know about him?"

"I saw you with him at the Salty Dog the other day," I said. "I did some research and figured out who he was."

"How?"

"I'll tell you when I come to see you. Can you eat yet?"

"They say I can," she said. "So yes."

"What kind of cookies do you like?"

"Um... lemon?" she said. "I barely know you, and you're bringing me cookies?"

"I found you half-dead on a beach," I said. "Of course I'm bringing you cookies! What room are you in?"

She gave me the details, and I hung up a moment later. "Now. Can we go back to the store?" I asked Nicholas.

"I think these people want to talk to you first," he said, gesturing toward Detective Andrews, who was standing about ten feet away eyeing me.

"All right," I said. "But next stop is my place. Will you come with me?"

"Of course," he said. "But we need to talk about this penchant of yours for running off into dangerous situations."

"Got it," I said as the detective walked over.

~

WE GOT to the shop just as Bethany was setting up for the reading. A woman with pale blonde hair was fussing with the chairs Bethany had put out, looking like she was preparing to face a firing line rather than a bunch of interested readers.

"How's it going?" I asked Bethany as she finished arranging a stack of books for the author, a women's fiction writer named Margaret Buxton, to sign.

"She's so nervous I'm afraid she's going to have a heart attack," Bethany murmured. "Her husband is here trying to get her to relax, but it isn't working so far; he just seems to be making her more upset." Devin was behind her, helping break down a box; I smiled at him, and he gave me a little wave back.

"Thanks for helping," I told him.

"I like helping Bethany... and supporting the store," he said.

"Where's Caroline?" I asked Bethany.

"She's taking a shower; she'll be down in a few," Bethany said. I was going to have to do something about the situation soon, I decided. It wasn't fair for Bethany to have to pick up all the slack.

As I was pondering my daughter, I heard a voice behind me.

"You're not going to choke," a man said.

"There's not going to be anyone here to choke for," a

woman's voice said, thin and anxious.

I spun around and my mouth dropped open. I recognized those voices! It was the couple I'd heard on the shore path the other day. They hadn't been talking about murder —they'd been talking about a book signing!

I walked over with a smile on my face. "You must be Margaret," I said. "Thank you so much for coming to do the signing! It's early yet; I'm sure it will fill up as we get closer to time."

"I don't know," she said. "These things make me so nervous."

"I'm sure you'll do great," I said, then turned to introduce myself to her husband, a tall, thin, stern-looking, brown-haired man with a sheaf of papers in his hand. "I'm Max. Max Sayers."

"John Buxton," he said. "Margaret's husband."

"How lovely that you're with her! Are you in town for a few days, then? Doing some sightseeing while you're here?" I asked them both as Margaret wrung her thin hands.

"We're staying with an old college friend off the shore path," he said. "I was hoping the sea air would help us figure out Margaret's next book and settle her nerves, but..."

"I'm an introvert, John," she said with a nervous laugh. "The only thing that's going to settle my nerves is not doing signings."

"Margaret..." he began.

"Can I get you a drink, or maybe a few cookies?" I offered, interrupting the lecture before it could begin. I'd pulled a double-batch of chocolate chip cookies out of the freezer earlier that day, and was planning to go and retrieve them and plate them if Caroline didn't emerge soon.

"Cookies might help," she said. "And maybe a cup of tea."

"The caffeine..." John cautioned.

"I'll make decaf," I said, heading up the stairs, relieved that at least one murder plot was fictional. I was two for two today. If the bookstore didn't work out, maybe I should take up private investigating.

My phone buzzed; it was Nicholas.

"Doing okay?" he asked.

"About to host a signing," I said.

"You up for an early morning treasure hunt tomorrow?" he asked.

"Of course!" I said.

"I'll meet you at eight," he said. "Don't worry... I'll bring coffee."

"You'd better," I said, feeling a zing of anticipation as I hung up and headed into the kitchen to put the kettle on and retrieve the cookies. Maybe we'd solve the third mystery tomorrow. Aren't good things supposed to come in threes?

BETHANY and I were sitting in two squashy chairs in the bookshop, relaxing after the book signing, and I had just finished telling her the whole story when Denise burst into the front door.

"I've got great news!" she announced, beaming.

"What's up?" I asked.

"I'm no longer a suspect! And Margaret is now offering to sell the store to me... but I don't think I'm going to buy it."

"What? Why not?"

"Because of the way she treated me the last few days; I don't trust her anymore and I'm not making any deals with her. But more importantly, because I'm going to open my own store! I'm going to look into leasing that building next door. I figure if you can do it, why can't I?"

I stood up. "Seriously?"

"Seriously," she said.

"Congratulations!" I said, and pulled her into a big hug. "I'm so happy for you!"

"I feel like a huge weight has been lifted off of me," she said. "The only thing is, I don't know why they suddenly decided I wasn't a suspect."

"I think Max can shed a little bit of light on that," Bethany said, and I told the story all over again.

THE NEXT MORNING was a quintessential Maine morning. The sky was cerulean blue dotted with puffy white clouds, the breeze was gentle and scented with salt water, balsam, and roses, and gulls cried overhead as they followed a fishing boat out to sea. Caroline had gone back to my mother's for the night, leaving me time to make a batch of lemon cookies and tidy the place before bed, and everything was feeling fresh and full of hope.

Nicholas appeared at my door at eight on the dot, a travel mug of coffee in hand. "Good morning, beautiful!" he said, and gave me a quick kiss. His clean, warm scent melted me, and I felt my heart patter at the thought of a morning on the boat with him; I'd left the store to Caroline to open this morning, and if she didn't show up, we'd have words later; I wasn't going to rescue her this time. "Ready?"

"Let me get the scones I made last night, and we'll be off," I said. "Thanks for the coffee!"

"Signing go okay?" he asked as I retrieved the Tupperware of scones.

"We had about twenty people, sold about ten of her books and fifteen other books, and the author didn't have a nervous breakdown, so I count it a success. Plus, I solved another mystery."

"Oh, really? Do tell!"

As we got into his car and headed to the dock where he kept his boat, I shared what I'd discovered about the people I'd overheard on the shore path; that they weren't actually talking about choking someone, but about choking during a reading.

He barked out a laugh. "You're kidding me!"

"Nope. They're staying at a friend's house for the week. I just happened to overhear them while they were out 'taking the sea air.'"

"Too funny," he said, then put his warm hand on mine. "Have you recovered from yesterday? It was a rough one. I don't like coming that close to losing you." He gave my hand a squeeze.

"I'm just glad Amanda's okay and Denise is no longer a suspect."

"Me too," he said. "Do you really think she'll set up shop next to you?"

"I hope so," I said. "I think we could really help each other out with marketing and traffic... and it would be great to be in the small-business-owner thing with my best friend."

"I'm so glad you moved to Snug Harbor," he said, and again, that warm feeling rushed through me.

"Me too," I said, giving him a peck on the cheek and taking a swig of my coffee. "Now. What's on our agenda for the day?"

"I found a coordinate in a weird spot," he said. "It only appears once, and it was written sideways right in the middle of the book. I thought we'd try it out."

"Sounds good to me," I said as we pulled in near the dock.

A half hour later, we were motoring across the broad sweep of dark blue water in Nicholas's motor boat, passing Eider ducks and a rainbow of lobster buoys as we headed in the direction of the coordinates he had found. I sat snuggled in next to him as we skimmed across the smooth water, the wind in our faces.

"Where is it?" I asked, leaning into him.

"It's on Pincushion Island."

"Pincushion Island?"

"It's a very small, uninhabited island," he said.

"Who knew?"

"Josiah Satterthwaite, evidently," he said, and I laughed.

"At least it isn't a big island," I said.

"I mapped it on my GPS app, and it will work even if we're out of service," he said. "Plus, I brought the topo map and my compass."

"You're a regular boy scout!" I said.

"Maybe you should follow my lead next time you go out on a boat," he said, grinning at me, but sounding rather serious. "I don't want to lose you." He put his arm around me and gave me a tight hug, and I nuzzled into his shoulder, feeling—for the first time in a very long time—like I was with someone who really was in my corner.

Before long, we were closing in on a very small, rocky island covered in trees that did, I had to admit, look a little like pins sticking out of a cushion. "I see why it's named Pincushion Island," I said as Nicholas let up on the throttle. "Where do we tie up?"

"I don't know yet, but there must be someplace," he said, slowing the boat and rounding the small island.

It didn't take long before I spotted the remains of a dock in a small inlet. "There," I said, pointing.

"Not much left," he said. "I hope we can tie up safely."

"I'll put out the bumpers; there are still a few planks in the dock. If they'll hold us, we should be okay."

He steered us expertly toward the weathered boards. I tied the small craft to the two piers, which didn't wobble when I tested them, and he cut the engine and nodded to me. "Good job. I'll go first, just in case the boards are too rotten."

"Be careful," I warned him as he stepped gingerly on the boards and then hopped to the flat rock a few feet past them.

"It feels sound, but grab my hand," he said, extending his arm to me. I grabbed it and leaped to shore, stepping only lightly on the ancient wood and grateful when my feet made contact with solid granite.

"We made it," I said. "Where do we go now?"

"Let me check," he said, pulling out his phone. "Looks like we go that way," he said, pointing up a rise that led through a tangle of low bushes studded with saplings and dead trees.

"Why are all the trees dead, do you think?"

"I don't know. Salt water, maybe?" he suggested as he pushed through the undergrowth. "No visible path here," he remarked. "Nobody's been here for a long time."

"Who do you think built that dock? Was the island inhabited?"

"I think some fishermen lived on the outer islands a long time ago, so they could be closer to the fishing grounds," he said, "but I couldn't find any record of any inhabitants here. Somebody had to build that dock, though."

"The rum runners?" I suggested.

"It's a good possibility," he agreed. "Although I only found one reference to this place in his notebook; I don't think it was a commonly used location, at least not for Satterthwaite and his crew." He glanced down at his phone as I stepped around a young fir tree. I passed the trunk of a long-dead tree and noticed the wood was blackened.

"I think there was a fire here," I said, pointing to the blackening I'd noticed, and then another a few feet behind it. "Look at these trees... the wood looks like charcoal."

"It's been a long time," he said, looking up at the tall, full-grown trees around us. "It's regrown well."

"I wonder what happened?" I asked.

He shrugged. "Lightning? Maybe whoever built that dock down there was still living here and accidentally caught the place on fire."

I shivered. "No fire department on call, a mile or two from land... that must have been terrifying. So much history here that we'll never know..."

"We're almost there," Nicholas said, interrupting my musing. "It should be... about ten feet in that direction."

I followed him until he stopped in a part of the wooded island that looked much like everything else we had walked through. "Now what?" I asked.

Nicholas stopped as if his toe hit against something, and then stooped. "Look," he said, pushing the leaf litter aside and exposing a line of granite rocks. "I think this is an old foundation."

"You're right!" I squatted down and began pushing away leaves; soon, we had exposed what was left of a foundation about ten feet by ten feet. "Must have burned in the fire."

"Which means whatever was in here burned, too, most likely," Nicholas said. "Maybe it's another dead end."

"Maybe," I said, "but we should look anyway." I began sifting through the dirt and leaf litter with the toe of my boot. "Since we came all this way."

"I'll start at this side and you start at that one," he said, going to one of the corners. I moved to the opposite corner and began looking through the inches of leaf litter that had collected over the years. If there had been a roof, it must have been shakes; there was no sign of burnt shingles, but I did find a few bits of melted glass.

"Windows?" I asked, "or dishware?"

"Either one," he said, holding up what appeared to be the rusty handle of a pot; the pot was long gone, either rusted out or separated from its handle. A few minutes later, he held up a hinge. "Wonder what this was?"

"I don't know," I said. A moment later, he found another one, and the remains of a lock.

"What, was it a treasure chest, or something?" Nicholas half-joked. "If so, whatever was in it is long gone."

"Let's look anyway," I said. I crouched next to him and kept pushing aside leaves and dirt, looking for anything that might have escaped the conflagration that had consumed what must have been a wooden or leather box, or trunk. As I dug through the dirt, my hand touched something cold and hard. "I've got something," I said, pushing away more dirt, then pulling my hand back.

"It's a gun," Nicholas said. "We have to be careful; it may still be loaded."

"Would it still work?"

"I'd rather not take chances," he said. As we cleared the rest of the dirt, Nicholas picked something up.

"What is it?"

"A key," he said, brushing off the dirt.

"Does it fit in the lock we found?"

He picked up the lock and attempted to slide the key in, then shook his head. "It's the wrong size," he said. "There's a little metal circle attached to it, with a number on it." He wiped off the dirt and held it up; the first line of numbers read 265. Underneath was the number 13.

"What could it be to?" I asked.

"I don't know," he said eyes twinkling, "but that's what we're going to find out!"

MURDER ON THE ROCKS CHAPTER ONE

Hungry for more Maine adventures? Escape to the Gray Whale Inn on quaint Cranberry Island, Maine!

Here's a sneak preview of the Agatha-nominated Murder on the Rocks, first in Karen's beloved ten-book (and counting) Gray Whale Inn cozy mystery series.

Chapter One

The alarm rang at 6 a.m., jolting me out from under my down comforter and into a pair of slippers. As much as I enjoyed innkeeping, I would never get used to climbing out of bed while everyone else was still sleeping. Ten minutes later I was in the kitchen, inhaling the aroma of dark-roasted coffee as I tapped it into the coffeemaker and gazing out the window at the gray-blue morning. Fog, it looked like —the swirling mist had swallowed even the Cranberry Rock lighthouse, just a quarter of a mile away. I grabbed the sugar and flour canisters from the pantry and dug a bag of blueberries out of the freezer for Wicked Blueberry Coffee Cake.

The recipe was one of my favorites: not only did my guests rave over the butter-and-brown-sugar-drenched cake, but its simplicity was a drowsy cook's dream.

The coffeepot had barely finished gurgling when I sprinkled the pan of dimpled batter with brown-sugar topping and eased it into the oven. My eyes focused on the clock above the sink: 6:30. Just enough time for a relaxed thirty minutes on the kitchen porch.

Equipped with a mug of steaming French-roast coffee, I grabbed my blue windbreaker from its hook next to the door and headed out into the gray Maine morning. As hard as it was to drag myself out of a soft, warm bed while it was still dark outside, I loved mornings on Cranberry Island.

I settled myself into a white-painted wooden rocker and took a sip of strong, sweet coffee. The sound of the waves crashing against the rocks was muted, but mesmerizing. I inhaled the tangy air as I rocked, watching the fog twirl around the rocks and feeling the kiss of a breeze on my cheeks. A tern wheeled overhead as the thrum of a lobster boat rumbled across the water, pulsing and fading as it moved from trap to trap.

"Natalie!" A voice from behind me shattered my reverie. I jumped at the sound of my name, spilling coffee on my legs. "I was looking for you." Bernard Katz's bulbous nose protruded from the kitchen door. I stood up and swiped at my coffee-stained jeans. I had made it very clear that the kitchen was off-limits to guests—not only was there a sign on the door, but it was listed in the house rules guests received when they checked in.

"Can I help you with something?" I couldn't keep the anger from seeping into my voice.

"We're going to need breakfast at seven. And my son and

his wife will be joining us. She doesn't eat any fat, so you'll have to have something light for her."

"But breakfast doesn't start until 8:30."

"Yes, well, I'm sure you'll throw something together." He glanced at his watch, a Rolex the size of a life preserver. "Oops! You'd better get cracking. They'll be here in twenty minutes."

I opened my mouth to protest, but he disappeared back into my kitchen with a bang. My first impulse was to storm through the door and tell Katz he could fish for his breakfast, but my business survival instinct kicked in. Breakfast at seven? Fine. That would be an extra $50 on his bill for the extra guests—and for the inconvenience. Scrambled egg whites should do the trick for Mrs. Katz Jr. First, however, a change of clothes was in order. I swallowed what was left of my coffee and took a deep, lingering breath of the salty air before heading inside to find a fresh pair of jeans.

My stomach clenched again as I climbed the stairs to my bedroom. Bernard Katz, owner of resorts for the rich and famous, had earmarked the beautiful, and currently vacant, fifty-acre parcel of land right next to the Gray Whale Inn for his next big resort—despite the fact that the Shoreline Conservation Association had recently reached an agreement with the Cranberry Island Board of Selectmen to buy the property and protect the endangered terns that nested there. The birds had lost most of their nesting grounds to people over the past hundred years, and the small strip of beach protected by towering cliffs was home to one of the largest tern populations still in existence.

Katz, however, was keen to make sleepy little Cranberry Island the next bijou in his crown of elite resorts, and was throwing bundles of money at the board to encourage them to sell it to him instead. If Katz managed to buy the land, I was afraid the sprawling resort would mean the end not only for the terns, but for the Gray Whale Inn.

As I reached the door to my bedroom, I wondered yet again why Katz and his assistant were staying at my inn. Bernard Katz's son Stanley and his daughter-in-law Estelle owned a huge "summer cottage" called Cliffside that was just on the other side of the preserve. I had been tempted to decline Katz's reservation, but the state of my financial affairs made it impossible to refuse any request for a week in two of my most expensive rooms.

I reminded myself that while Katz and his assistant Ogden Wilson were odious, my other guests—the Bittles, a retired couple up from Alabama for an artists' retreat—were lovely, and deserved a wonderful vacation. And at least Katz had paid up front. As of last Friday, my checking account had dropped to under $300, and the next mortgage payment was due in two weeks. Although Katz's arrival on the island might mean the eventual end of the Gray Whale Inn, right now I needed the cash.

Goosebumps crept up my legs under the wet denim as I searched for something to wear. Despite the fact that it was June, and one of the warmer months of the year, my body hadn't adjusted to Maine's lower temperatures. I had spent the last fifteen years under Austin's searing sun, working for the Texas Department of Parks and Wildlife and dreaming of someday moving to the coast to start a bed-and-breakfast.

I had discovered the Gray Whale Inn while staying with a friend in a house she rented every summer on Mount Desert Island. I had come to Maine to heal a broken heart, and had no idea I'd fall in love all over again—this time with a 150-year-old former sea captain's house on a small island accessible only by boat.

The inn was magical; light airy rooms with views of the

sea, acres of beach roses, and sweet peas climbing across the balconies. I jotted down the real estate agent's number and called on a whim, never guessing that my long-term fantasy might be within my grasp. When the agent informed me that the inn was for sale at a bargain price, I raced to put together enough money for a down payment.

I had had the good fortune to buy a large old house when Austin was a sleepy town in a slump. After a room-by-room renovation, it sold for three times the original price, and between the proceeds of the house and my entire retirement savings, there was just enough money to take out a mortgage on the inn. A mortgage, I reflected as I strained to button my last pair of clean jeans, whose monthly payments were equivalent to the annual Gross National Product of Sweden.

I tossed my coffee-stained jeans into the overflowing laundry basket and paused for a last-minute inspection in the cloudy mirror above the dresser. Gray eyes looked back at me from a face only slightly plump from two months of butter-and sugar-laden breakfasts and cookies. I took a few swipes at my bobbed brown hair with a brush and checked for white hairs—no new ones today, although with the Katzes around my hair might be solid white by the end of the summer. If I hadn't already torn all of my hair out, that is.

When I pushed through the swinging door to the dining room at 7:00, Bernard Katz sat alone, gazing out the broad sweep of windows toward the section of coastline he had earmarked for his golf course. He looked like a banker in a blue pinstriped three-piece suit whose buttons strained to cover his round stomach. Katz turned at the sound of my footsteps, exposing a line of crooked teeth as he smiled. He was a self-made man, someone had told me. Apparently there'd been no money in the family budget for orthodontic work. Still, if I had enough money to buy islands, I'd have found a couple of thousand dollars to spare for straight teeth.

"Coffee. Perfect." He plucked the heavy blue mug from the place setting in front of him and held it out. "I'll take cream and sugar." I filled his cup, congratulating myself for not spilling it on his pants, then plunked the cream pitcher and sugar bowl on the table.

"You know, you stand to earn quite a bit of business from our little project." Katz took a sip of coffee. "Not bad," he said, sounding surprised. "Anyway, there's always a bit of overflow in the busy season. We might be able to arrange something so that your guests could use our facilities. For a fee, of course."

Of course. He leaned back and put his expensively loafered feet on one of my chairs. Apparently he was willing to cough up some change for footwear. "I know starting a business is tough, and it looks like your occupancy is on the low side." He nodded at the room full of empty tables.

"Well, it is an hour and a half before breakfast." He didn't have to know that only two other rooms were booked —and one of those was for Barbara Eggleby, the Shoreline Conservation Association representative who was coming to the island for the sole purpose of preventing his development from happening.

"Still," he went on, "this is the high season." His eyes swept over the empty tables. "Or should be. Most of the inns in this area are booked to capacity." My first impulse was to respond that most of the inns in the area had been open for more than two months, and that he was welcome to go to the mainland and stay at one of them, but I held my tongue.

He removed his feet from my chair and leaned toward

me. "Our resort will make Cranberry Island *the* hot spot for the rich and famous in Maine. Kennebunkport won't know what hit it. Your place will be perfect for the people who want glitz but can't afford the price tag of the resort."

Glitz? The whole point of Cranberry Island was its ruggedness and natural beauty. So my inn would be a catchall for poor people who couldn't quite swing the gigantic tab at Katz's mega resort. Lovely.

I smiled. "Actually, I think the island works better as a place to get away from all the 'glitz'. And I don't think a golf course would do much to enhance the island's appeal." I paused for a moment. "Or the nesting success of the black-chinned terns."

"Oh, yes, the birds." He tsked and shook his head. The sun gleamed on his bald pate, highlighting the liver spots that had begun to appear like oversized freckles. "I almost forgot, you're heading up that greenie committee. I would have thought you were smarter than that, being a business-woman." He waved a hand. "Well, I'm sure we could work something out, you know, move the nests somewhere else or something."

"Good morning, Bernie." The sharp report of stiletto heels rescued me from having to respond. *Bernie?*

"Estelle!" Katz virtually leaped from his chair. "Please, sit down." Katz's daughter-in-law approached the table in a blaze of fuchsia and decorated Katz's cheeks with two air kisses before favoring him with a brilliant smile of straight, pearl-white teeth. Clearly orthodontic work had been a priority for her. Her frosted blonde hair was coiffed in a Marilyn Monroe pouf, and the neckline of her hot pink suit plunged low enough to expose a touch of black lace bra. An interesting choice for a foggy island morning on the coast of Maine. Maybe this was what Katz meant by glitz.

She turned her ice-blue eyes to me and arranged her frosted pink lips in a hard line. "Coffee. Black." She returned her gaze to Katz, composing her face into a simpering smile as he pulled out a chair for her.

"Estelle, I'm so glad you could come. Where's Stanley?" Stanley Katz was Bernard Katz's son, and Estelle's husband. I'd seen him around the island; he had inherited his father's girth and balding pate, but not his business sense or charisma. Stanley and Estelle had seemed like a mismatched couple to me until I found out the Katzes were rolling in the green stuff. As much as I didn't like the Katzes, I felt sorry for Stanley. Between his overbearing father and his glamorous wife, he faded into the background.

"Stanley?" Estelle looked like she was searching her brain to place the name. "Oh, he's out parking the car. I didn't want to have to walk over all of those horrid rocks." She fixed me with a stare. "You really should build a proper walkway. I could have broken a heel."

Katz chuckled. "When the Cranberry Island Premier Resort is built, you won't have to worry about any rocks, my dear." Or birds, or plants, or anything else that was "inconvenient." Their voices floated over my shoulder as I headed back to the kitchen. "You look stunning as usual, Estelle."

"Keep saying things like that and I'll be wishing I'd married *you*!" I rolled my eyes as the kitchen door swung shut behind me. The aroma of coffee cake enveloped me as I ran down my mental checklist. Fruit salad, whole wheat toast, and skinny scrambled eggs for Estelle; scrambled whole eggs and blueberry coffee cake would work for Katz, who from the bulge over his pin-striped pants didn't seem too interested in Weight Watchers-style breakfasts. I tugged at the snug waistband of my jeans and grimaced. At least

Katz and I had one thing in common. I grabbed a crystal bowl from the cabinet and two melons from the countertop.

As the French chef's knife sliced through the orange flesh of a cantaloupe, my eyes drifted to the window. I hoped the blanket of fog would lift soon. The Cranberry Island Board of Selectmen was meeting tonight to decide what to do with the land next door, and Barbara Eggleby, the Shoreline Conservation Association representative, was due in today. I was afraid the bad weather might delay her flight. *Save Our Terns*, the three-person island group I had formed to save the terns' nesting ground from development, was counting on Barbara for the financial backing to combat Katz's bid for development. As I slid melon chunks into the bowl and retrieved a box of berries from the refrigerator, my eyes returned to the window. The fog did look like it was letting up a bit. I could make out a lobster boat chugging across the leaden water. The berries tumbled into a silver colander like dark blue and red gems, and as the water from the faucet gushed over them, the small boat paused to haul a trap. A moment later, the engine growled as the boat turned and steamed toward the mainland, threading its way through the myriad of brightly colored buoys that studded the cold saltwater.

Since moving to the island, I had learned that each lobsterman had a signature buoy color that enabled him to recognize his own traps, as well as the traps of others. I had been surprised to discover that what I thought of as open ocean was actually carved up into unofficial but zealously guarded fishing territories.

My eyes followed the receding boat as I gave the berries a final swirl and turned off the faucet. Lately, some of the lobstermen from the mainland had been encroaching on island territory, and the local lobster co-op was in an uproar.

I strained my eyes to see if any of the offending red and green buoys were present. The veil of fog thinned for a moment, and sure enough, bobbing next to a jaunty pink and white one was a trio of what looked like nautical Christmas ornaments.

The boat had vanished from sight by the time the fruit salad was finished. I eyed my creation—the blueberries and raspberries interspersed with the bright green of kiwi made a perfect complement to the cantaloupe—and opened the fridge to retrieve a dozen eggs and some fat-free milk. When I turned around, I slammed into Ogden Wilson, Katz's skinny assistant. My fingers tightened on the milk before it could slip from my grasp, but the impact jolted the eggs out of my hand. I stifled a curse as the carton hit the floor. Was I going to have to install a lock on the kitchen door?

Ogden didn't apologize. Nor did he stoop to help me collect the egg carton, which was upended in a gelatinous mess on my hardwood floor. "Mr. Katz would like to know when breakfast will be ready." His eyes bulged behind the thick lenses of his glasses. With his oily pale skin and lanky body, he reminded me of some kind of cave-dwelling amphibian. I wished he'd crawl back into his hole.

I bent down to inventory the carton; only three of the dozen had survived. "Well, now that we're out of eggs, it will be a few minutes later." It occurred to me that I hadn't considered him when doing the breakfast tally. Although Ogden generally stuck to his boss like glue, it was easy to forget he existed. "Are you going to be joining them?"

"Of course. But do try to hurry. Mr. Katz has an extremely busy schedule."

"Well, I'm afraid breakfast will be slightly delayed." I tipped my chin toward the mess on the floor. "But I'll see what I can do."

The oven timer buzzed as Ogden slipped through the swinging door to the dining room. I rescued the cake from the oven and squatted to clean up the mess on the floor. What kind of urgent business could Bernard Katz have on an island of less than a square mile? Most of the movers and shakers here were fishermen's wives after a few too many beers. I hoped Barbara Eggleby would be able to convince the board that the Shoreline Conservation Association was the right choice for the land next door. The Katz development would be a cancer on the island. Lord knew the Katzes were.

I raced up the stairs and knocked on my niece's door. Gwen had come to work with me for the summer, cleaning the rooms, covering the phones, and helping with the cooking from time to time in exchange for room and board. The help was a godsend— not only was it free, but it allowed me time to work on promoting the inn—but Gwen was not a perfect assistant.

Part of the reason Gwen was spending the summer at the inn was that her mother didn't know what else to do with her: she'd flunked half of her classes her first year at UCLA and my sister couldn't spend more than ten minutes in the same room with her daughter without one or the other of them declaring war. Her work at the inn, while not F-level, was between a B and a C, when I needed everything to be A+. Still, help was help, and beggars couldn't be choosers. I wished that some of the enthusiasm she showed for the art classes she was taking on the island would spill over to her housekeeping skills.

"Who is it?" answered a groggy voice from the other side of the door. I cracked the door open. Gwen's hair was a messy brown halo in the dim light from the curtained window.

"I'm sorry to wake you, but I need you to run down to Charlene's and get a dozen eggs."

"What time is it?"

"It's just after seven. Please hurry... I've got guests waiting."

She groaned. "Seven in the *morning*?"

"I know. But it's an emergency." She grumbled something and began to move toward the side of the bed, so I closed the door and jogged back down the stairs. I'd start with fruit salad and a plate of coffee cake, and bring out the eggs later. Maybe a pan of sausage, too... I could keep it warm until the Bittles came down at 8:30.

I was retrieving a package of pork sausages from the freezer when someone tapped on the door to the back porch. I whirled around to tell the Katzes I'd meet them in the dining room shortly, and saw the sun-streaked brown hair of my neighbor, John Quinton. "Come in!" I hollered, smiling for the first time that morning.

John's green eyes twinkled in a face already brown from afternoons out on the water in his sailboat, and his faded green T-shirt and shorts were streaked with sawdust. John was both a friend and a tenant; he rented the inn's converted carriage house from me, as well as a small shed he had converted to a workshop. He was a sculptor who created beautiful things from the driftwood that washed up on the beaches, but supplemented what he called his "art habit" with a variety of part-time jobs. In the spring and summer, he made toy sailboats for the gift shop on the pier. He also held a year-round job as the island's only deputy.

"You're up early. Working on a new project?" I asked.

"Island Artists ordered a few more boats. I figured I'd churn them out this morning and then start on some fun stuff." His eyes glinted with mischief. "One of Claudette's goats was eyeing your sweet peas, by the way. I shooed her off, but I'm afraid she'll be back."

I groaned. Claudette White was one of the three members of *Save Our Terns*, and was known on the island as "eccentric." Although her husband, Eleazer, was a boat-builder and popular with the locals, most of the islanders gave Claudette a wide berth. Her goats were almost as unpopular as she was, since they were notorious for escaping and consuming other people's gardens.

When Claudette wasn't caring for her goats or knitting their wool into sweaters and hats, she was holding forth at length about the evils of the modern world to anyone who would listen. I wasn't delighted that she had chosen to join *Save Our Terns*, but since the only other takers had been my best friend, Charlene, and me, we didn't feel we could turn her down.

John watched me pry sausage links out of a box and into a cast-iron pan. "I'm not the only one up early. I thought breakfast wasn't till 8:30."

"Yeah, well, we're working on Katz time today." A thump came from overhead, and then the sound of the shower. I sighed: so much for urgency. Gwen must be performing her morning ablutions. I appealed to John for help. "Do you have any eggs I can borrow? I was going to send Gwen down to the store, but I'm short on time."

"I just picked up a dozen yesterday. Is that enough?"

"You're a lifesaver." He disappeared through the back door, and the thought flitted through my mind that he might stay for a cup of coffee when he got back. I spooned fruit salad into a crystal bowl and reminded myself that John had a girlfriend in Portland. Five minutes later I sailed into the dining room bearing the fruit salad and a platter mounded with hot coffee cake. Stanley Katz had arrived, and sat hunched in an ill-fitting brown suit next to his wife. Estelle glared at me. "Coffee cake? I can't eat that. I thought this breakfast was supposed to be low-fat!" Then she pointed a lacquered nail at the ginger-colored cat who had curled up in a sunbeam on the windowsill. "And why is there a *cat* in your dining room? Surely that's against health department regulations?"

I scooped up Biscuit and deposited her in the living room. She narrowed her gold-green eyes at me and stalked over to the sofa as I hurried back into the dining room. "I'll have skinny scrambled eggs and wheat toast out shortly," I said. "We had a slight mishap in the kitchen." I shot Ogden a look. He blinked behind his thick lenses. I attempted a bright smile. "Can I get anybody more coffee?"

Estelle sighed. "I suppose so." She turned to her father-in-law, who had already transferred two pieces of cake to his plate. "With this kind of service," she muttered under her breath, "I don't know how she expects to stay in business."

When I got back into the kitchen, a carton of eggs lay on the butcher-block counter. Darn. I'd missed John. The sausages had started to sizzle and Estelle's egg whites were almost done when the phone rang.

"Nat."

"Charlene? You're up early." Charlene was the local grocer, a fellow member of *Save Our Terns*, and my source for island gossip. She was also my best friend.

"I've got bad news."

I groaned. "You're kidding. The Katzes sprang a surprise 7 a.m. breakfast on me and then his assistant broke all of my eggs. It can't get any worse."

"It can. I just talked to the coastal airport: no planes in or out, probably for the whole day. A big nor'easter is about to hit the coast."

My heart thumped in my chest. "The airport is closed? So Barbara isn't going to make it in time for the council meeting?"

"It's just you and me, babe. And Claudette."

My stomach sank. Without a representative from the Shoreline Conservation Association to combat Katz's offer for the property next to the inn, we could only sit and watch as Katz wooed the board of selectmen with visions of the fat bank accounts the island would enjoy when the Cranberry Island Premier Resort came into being.

I leaned my head against the wall. "We're sunk."

Download your copy of Murder on the Rocks now to find out what happens next!

Praise for the Gray Whale Inn mysteries...

"**This book is an absolute gem.**" — Suspense Magazine

"Deliciously clever plot. Juicy characters. Karen MacInerney has cooked up a winning recipe for murder. **Don't miss this mystery!**" — *New York Times* Bestselling Author Maggie Sefton

"...a new **cozy author worth investigating.**" — Publishers Weekly

"Murder on the Rocks mixes a pinch of salt air, a hunky love interest, an island divided by environmental issues... and, of course, murder. **Add Karen MacInerney to your list of favorite Maine mystery authors.**" — Lea Wait, author of the Antique Print mystery series

"**Sure to please cozy readers.**" — Library Journal

"I look anxiously forward to the sequel... Karen MacInerney has a **winning recipe for a great series.**" — Julie Obermiller, Features Editor, Mysterical-E

MORE BOOKS BY KAREN MACINERNEY

To download a free book and receive members-only outtakes, giveaways, short stories, recipes, and updates, join Karen's Reader's Circle at <u>www.karenmacinerney.com</u>! You can also join her Facebook community; she often hosts giveaways and loves getting to know her readers there.

And don't forget to follow her on BookBub to get newsflashes on new releases!

The Snug Harbor Mysteries
A Killer Ending
Inked Out
The Lies that Bind
Snug Harbor Cozy Mystery #4 (Coming 2023)

The Gray Whale Inn Mysteries
Murder on the Rocks
Dead and Berried
Murder Most Maine

Berried to the Hilt
Brush With Death
Death Runs Adrift
Whale of a Crime
Claws for Alarm
Scone Cold Dead
Anchored Inn
Gray Whale Inn Mystery #11 (Coming 2023)
Cookbook: The Gray Whale Inn Kitchen
Four Seasons of Mystery (A Gray Whale Inn Collection)
Blueberry Blues (A Gray Whale Inn Short Story)
Pumpkin Pied (A Gray Whale Inn Short Story)
Iced Inn (A Gray Whale Inn Short Story)
Lupine Lies (A Gray Whale Inn Short Story)

The Dewberry Farm Mysteries

Killer Jam
Fatal Frost
Deadly Brew
Mistletoe Murder
Dyeing Season
Wicked Harvest
Sweet Revenge
Peach Clobber
Dewberry Farm Mystery #9 (Coming 2023)
Slay Bells Ring: A Dewberry Farm Christmas Story
Cookbook: Lucy's Farmhouse Kitchen

The Margie Peterson Mysteries

Mother's Day Out
Mother Knows Best
Mother's Little Helper

Wolves and the City

> *Howling at the Moon*
> *On the Prowl*
> *Leader of the Pack*

RECIPES

MISSISSIPPI MUD BARS

Ingredients:

For the brownies:

- 1/3 cup unsweetened cocoa powder
- 1 cup butter, softened
- 2 cups granulated sugar
- 4 large eggs
- 2 teaspoons vanilla extract
- 1 1/2 cups all-purpose flour
- 1 teaspoon salt
- 3 cups mini marshmallows
- 1 cup nuts (optional)

For the frosting:

- 1/2 cup butter, melted
- 1/3 cup unsweetened cocoa powder
- 1/3 cup evaporated milk
- 1 teaspoon vanilla extract

- 3 - 3 1/2 cups powdered sugar

Directions:

For the brownies:
- Preheat oven to 350 degrees F and grease a 9x13" pan.
- In a large mixing bowl, mix cocoa and softened butter and mix until smooth. Add sugar and mix for 1 minute. Add eggs, one at a time, mixing after each addition. Add vanilla and mix.
- Add flour and salt and stir to combine. Add nuts if using.
- Pour batter into prepared pan. Bake for 25-30 minutes or until a toothpick inserted into the center comes out clean.
- Remove brownies from the oven and sprinkle the marshmallows evenly on top. Return to the oven for 2-3 minutes or until the marshmallows are puffed. Remove from oven and allow to cool completely. Once brownies are cool, make the frosting.

For the frosting:
- Add melted butter, cocoa powdered, evaporated milk, vanilla, and 2 cups of powdered sugar to a mixing bowl and beat with electric beaters until smooth.
- Add more powdered sugar, a cup at a time, mixing well, until frosting is thick enough to spread easily but not too liquid (approximately 3 1/4 cups powdered sugar).
- Spread frosting over the cooled brownies and cut into squares.

BLUEBERRY BOY BAIT

Ingredients:

For the streusel topping:

- 6 tablespoons packed light brown sugar
- 1/2 cup all-purpose flour
- 1 teaspoon ground cinnamon
- 1/4 teaspoon salt
- 4 tablespoons cold butter, cut into 1/2-inch chunks

For the cake:

- 2 cups all-purpose flour
- 2 teaspoons baking powder
- 1/2 teaspoon salt
- 1 stick unsalted butter, softened
- 3/4 cup granulated sugar
- 2 eggs
- 1-1/2 teaspoons vanilla extract

- I teaspoon lemon zest
- 1/2 cup milk
- 2 cups fresh or frozen blueberries

Directions:

. Make the streusel topping by combining the brown sugar, flour, cinnamon, and salt in a small bowl. Whisk with a fork until no lumps of brown sugar remain, then rub in the butter with your fingertips until it reaches a crumbly state. Refrigerate until ready to use.

. Preheat the oven to 375°F and set an oven rack in the center of the oven. Grease a 9-inch square pan.

. In a medium bowl, whisk together the flour, baking powder and salt, and set aside.

. In a large bowl, beat the butter and granulated sugar until creamy, about 2 minutes. Add the eggs one at a time, scraping down the sides of the bowl and beating well after each addition. Beat in the vanilla extract and lemon zest.

. Gradually add the flour mixture to the butter mixture, alternating with the milk, beating on low speed until combined. Then add the berries to the batter and fold gently with a spatula until evenly distributed. Do not over-mix.

. Transfer the batter to prepared pan and spread evenly, then sprinkle streusel topping evenly over the batter. Bake for 40 to 45 minutes, until golden brown around the edges and a toothpick comes out clean.

LUSCIOUS LEMON COOKIES

Ingredients:

For the cookies:

- 1 cup unsalted butter (softened)
- 1 cup confectioners' sugar
- 1 tablespoon lemon zest (finely grated)
- 1 ½ tablespoons lemon juice (freshly squeezed)
- 2 cups all-purpose flour
- ¾ teaspoon kosher salt

For the glaze:

- ½ cup plus 2 tablespoons confectioners' sugar
- 1 tablespoon fresh lemon juice
- 1 tablespoon unsoftened butter
- Lemon zest (for garnish)

Directions:

For the cookies:

- Preheat the oven to 350° and set racks in the upper and lower thirds.
- In a large bowl, beat the butter with the confectioners' sugar until very smooth.
- Beat in the lemon zest and juice, then beat in the flour and salt until just mixed; scrape down the side of the bowl as necessary.
- Roll half of the dough into 1-inch balls and arrange the balls 1 inch apart on 2 baking sheets. Flatten cookies gently with the bottom of a glass.
- Bake cookies for 12 to 14 minutes, until they are lightly brown on the bottom and just firm. Switch the baking sheets from top to bottom and front to back halfway through baking.
- Let the cookies cool on the baking sheets for 2 minutes before transferring to a rack to cool completely.
- Repeat with the remaining dough.

For the glaze:

- In a bowl, whisk the confectioners' sugar with the lemon juice and butter until smooth.
- Spread the lemon glaze on the cooled cookies and garnish with finely grated lemon zest.

ABOUT THE AUTHOR

Karen is the housework-impaired, award-winning author of multiple mystery series, and her victims number well into the double digits. She lives in Austin, Texas with her sassy family, Tristan, and Little Bit (a.k.a. Dog #1 and Dog #2).

Feel free to visit Karen's web site, where you can download a free book and sign up for her Readers' Circle to receive subscriber-only short stories, deleted scenes, recipes and other bonus material. You can also find her on Facebook (she spends an inordinate amount of time there), where Karen loves getting to know her readers, answering questions, and offering quirky, behind-the-scenes looks at the writing process (and life in general). And please follow her on Bookbub to find out about new releases and sales!

P. S. Don't forget to follow Karen on BookBub to get news-flashes on new releases!

www.karenmacinerney.com
karen@karenmacinerney.com

facebook.com/AuthorKarenMacInerney
twitter.com/KarenMacInerney

CPSIA information can be obtained
at www.ICGtesting.com
Printed in the USA
BVHW031015190123
656634BV00005B/87